DYNASTIES

Seven Sins

One man's betrayal can destroy generations.

Ten years ago, a hedge-fund hotshot vanished with billions, leaving the high-powered families of Falling Brook changed forever.

Now seven heirs, shaped by his betrayal, must reckon with the sins of the past.

Passion may be their only path to redemption.

Experience all Seven Sins!

* * *

Ruthless Pride by Naima Simone

This CEO's pride led him to give up his dreams for his family. Now he's drawn to the woman who threatens everything...

Forbidden Lust by Karen Booth

He's always resisted his lust for his best friend's sister—until they're stranded together in paradise...

Insatiable Hunger by Yahrah St. John

His unbridled appetite for his closest friend is unleashed when he believes she's fallen for the wrong man...

Hidden Ambition by Jules Bennett

Ambition has taken him far, but revenge could cost him his one chance at love...

Reckless Envy by Joss Wood

When this shark in the boardroom meets the one woman he can't have, envy takes over...

Untamed Passion by Cat Schield

Will this black sheep's self-destructive wrath flame out when he's expecting an heir of his own?

Slow Burn by Janice Maynard

If he's really the idle playboy his family claims, will his inaction threaten a reunion with the woman who got away?

"I want you, Zane. All of you."

"I can't give you that. Not now."

"Then when? Later tonight? Tomorrow morning? Please don't tell me we're going to leave this island without having sex." Allison wanted to applaud herself for truly putting it all out there.

"I've thought about it and it's not a good idea. We've already gone too far."

She knew what that really meant.

"Nobody needs to know about this, Zane. Nobody. I don't kiss and tell. And I certainly wouldn't kiss and tell about you."

Zane turned away. "I would know it had happened. That's all that matters."

* * *

Forbidden Lust by Karen Booth is part of the Dynasties: Seven Sins series.

KAREN BOOTH

FORBIDDEN LUST

HARLEQUIN
DESIRE

If you purchased this book without a cover you should be aware
that this book is stolen property. It was reported as "unsold and
destroyed" to the publisher, and neither the author nor the
publisher has received any payment for this "stripped book."

For the members of the Backstage Antics with Karen
crew on Facebook. You guys are the absolute best!

Special thanks and acknowledgment are given
to Karen Booth for her contribution to the
Dynasties: Seven Sins miniseries.

HARLEQUIN®
DESIRE™

Recycling programs
for this product may
not exist in your area.

ISBN-13: 978-1-335-20914-6

Forbidden Lust

Copyright © 2020 by Harlequin Books S.A.

All rights reserved. No part of this book may be used or reproduced in any
manner whatsoever without written permission except in the case of brief
quotations embodied in critical articles and reviews.

This is a work of fiction. Names, characters, places and incidents
are either the product of the author's imagination or are used fictitiously.
Any resemblance to actual persons, living or dead, businesses,
companies, events or locales is entirely coincidental.

This edition published by arrangement with Harlequin Books S.A.

For questions and comments about the quality of this book,
please contact us at CustomerService@Harlequin.com.

Harlequin Enterprises ULC
22 Adelaide St. West, 40th Floor
Toronto, Ontario M5H 4E3, Canada
www.Harlequin.com

Printed in U.S.A.

Karen Booth is a Midwestern girl transplanted in the South, raised on '80s music and repeated readings of *Forever* by Judy Blume. When she takes a break from the art of romance, she's listening to music with her college-aged kids or sweet-talking her husband into making her a cocktail. Learn more about Karen at karenbooth.net.

Books by Karen Booth

Harlequin Desire

The Eden Empire

A Christmas Temptation
A Cinderella Seduction
A Bet with Benefits
A Christmas Seduction
A Christmas Rendezvous

Dynasties: Secrets of the A-List

Tempted by Scandal

Dynasties: Seven Sins

Forbidden Lust

Visit her Author Profile page at Harlequin.com, or karenbooth.net, for more titles.

You can find Karen Booth on Facebook, along with other Harlequin Desire authors, at Facebook.com/harlequindesireauthors!

Dear Reader,

Thanks for picking up *Forbidden Lust*! I loved writing this book because it was yet another chance for me to explore two of my favorite romance tropes—unrequited love and the best friend's younger sister. Both themes are so much fun!

Zane and Allison have known each other since Zane's life fell apart in the aftermath of the Black Crescent scandal. Allison was a few years younger and developed a massive crush on Zane that never quite went away. Even all these years later, her lust for him is still bubbling under the surface. He's just too sexy and brooding for her to stay away. Zane never dared to think about Allison that way when they were in high school, but now that they're both grown up, it's impossible to ignore the beautiful, vibrant woman she has become.

Enter Allison's brother, Scott. Zane is indebted to Scott for standing by him during the most difficult time of his life. Scott is incredibly protective of Allison, who went through a scary illness when she was a young girl. Scott doesn't want Zane and Allison within fifty feet of each other, let alone stuck on a remote Bahamian island together...but sometimes a hurricane rolls in and there's nothing to do but ride out the storm! I think it made for a sexy, emotional story with lots of ups and downs.

I sincerely hope you enjoy Dynasties: Seven Sins and continue to read through the series. There are so many fabulous authors to discover. In the meantime, drop me a line anytime at karen@karenbooth.net. I love hearing from readers!

Karen

One

Zane Patterson's heart was hammering. His T-shirt was soaked with sweat, clinging to his shoulders. "I need to get out of this town. That's all there is to it." He dribbled the basketball with his right hand. *Thump. Thump. Thump.* Switching to his left, Zane waited for his opening—his chance to drive past his best friend, Scott Randall. Their weekly game of one-on-one was tied. One more point and victory was Zane's. So very close. He did not like to lose. He hated it.

"Dude. You've been saying that since high school. It's been fifteen years." Laser-focused on Zane's every move, Scott shuffled from side to side, hands high, low and anywhere Zane dared to even think about looking. Scott didn't allow himself to get distracted by the perspiration raining down from the top of his shiny bald head. He only cared about not giving up the final point. "You either need to leave or get over it."

The reason for leaving—Joshua Lowell—popped into Zane's head. Zane despised him. He had the smuggest smile, like he was perfectly comfortable with the silver spoon firmly lodged in his mouth at birth. The entirety of Falling Brook, New Jersey, put that jerk on a pedestal, even when his father had destroyed lives and families, including Zane's. Deep down, Zane loved his hometown, but being here was pushing him closer and closer to the edge. *Get over it? No way.*

Thump. He palmed the ball. *Thump.* Left. *Thump.* Right. *Thump.* Back left. He dropped his shoulder, slipped around Scott and beelined for the basket. With Scott in hot pursuit but several strides behind him, Zane finger-rolled the ball for a layup. It circled the rim. And popped back out. Scott grabbed the rebound, spun away from Zane and hoisted up a perfect jumper. Nothing but net.

Dammit.

"Yes!" Scott darted under the basket and snatched the ball. "Rematch? Best two out of three?"

Zane bent over, clutching the hem of his basketball shorts and planting the heels of his hands on his knees. "No." The competitive part of him wanted the win. Needed it. Playing basketball was one of the only activities that had ever made him happy. He'd been at it since he could walk, precisely the reason he had an indoor court installed when his company, Patterson Marketing, took off and they built their own state-of-the-art office building. But he was too exhausted to compete. Or fight. Mentally, more than anything. "I'm done."

"This Joshua Lowell thing is really getting to you, isn't it?" Scott rested the ball on his hip, letting the weight of his forearm hold it in place.

"I can't get away from it. The anniversary article was supposed to remind everyone what crooks the Lowells are, how they destroyed lives, how they can never be trusted. Instead, Josh's engagement to Sophie Armstrong is all anyone is talking about. It's everywhere. Facebook. Twitter. The Java Hut. My own freaking staff meeting."

"It's a big deal. He's stepping away from BC. Nobody saw that coming."

BC. The initials for Black Crescent were enough to make Zane cringe. The hedge fund, founded by Joshua Lowell's father, Vernon, had been an ultraexclusive avenue of investment for the superrich. Zane's family had once breathed the rarefied air of those on the limited client list, and for a time, the world was sunshine and roses. There was no shortage of money, and Zane's life was golden—king of the school at Falling Brook Prep, captain of the basketball team, parents happily married. Then Vernon disappeared with millions, Zane's family was left penniless and his parents' marriage was destroyed.

Losing their family fortune meant that Zane had been moved from Prep to the public high school at the age of sixteen. It was another brutal adjustment, especially since the kids at Falling Brook High treated Zane like the rich kid who needed to be taken down a notch or two. They had no idea Zane was already at rock bottom. The only consolation was that he'd met Scott there, and they'd been best friends ever since.

Scott saved Zane, mostly from himself. Scott didn't give a damn about the money; he only wanted to help, and he only wanted to be friends. They were solid from day one. When Zane's mom and dad fought, which was often, Scott's parents allowed Zane to seek refuge at their house. It was an oasis of calm—the one place happiness seemed possible. One of the best parts of those stays was spending time with Scott's younger sister, Allison. She was the coolest, smartest and most creative person Zane had ever met. She was supercute, too, but Zane had always looked past that. She was Scott's sister, and Zane would never, ever go there. Never.

"Did you see Josh's press conference? Did you hear what he said? 'She brought me out of the dark with her love'? 'Because she loves me, I am worthy'? What a load of crap." Zane didn't enjoy being so bitter, but the fifteen years since Vernon Lowell disappeared had done nothing to assuage his pain over his entire life crumbling to dust. As far as Zane was concerned, all Lowells—Vernon; his wife, Eve; and his kids, Joshua, Jake and Oliver—were pure poison. He didn't want to see any of them happy.

"You know what they say. Love makes everything better."

Zane shot Scott a look. Romantic love was a farce. It rarely, if ever, lasted. Zane's parents were a classic example. Yes, they'd been tested when Vernon Lowell stole every penny they had, but wasn't love supposed to conquer all? Not from where Zane was sitting. "Said like a very married man."

"Don't get salty because I'm happy. Last time I checked, there wasn't a law against it."

Zane grumbled under his breath. He didn't want to continue this part of their conversation.

The two men wandered over to the corner of the gym to grab the six-pack of microbrew Scott had stashed in the fully stocked beverage fridge. Zane was more of a tequila or mescal guy, but after a game, there was nothing better than knocking back a cold beer. They took it outside to the patio, where employees often enjoyed their lunch or an afternoon meeting if the weather was nice. A warm June night, the air was sweet and a bit heavy with humidity, but there was a pleasant breeze. Zane and Scott sat at a table, and Scott popped open the first two bottles. They clinked them to toast.

Zane took in a deep breath, washing down his resentment with that first sip of beer, trying to remind himself that he really did love it here. "I never should have gone to Joshua Lowell at the bar and told him I knew about the DNA report because I was the one who gave it to Sophie for the article about Black Crescent. I should have let him wonder who her sources were. I should have let him stew in his own juices. That's what he deserves." He took another long draw of his drink. That had been a difficult confrontation. Just seeing Joshua Lowell face-to-face was enough to make him physically ill. "I wanted him to know that he wasn't as high and mighty as everyone thought. That I knew who he really was."

Zane remembered the odd jolt that went through his body when he received the DNA report in the mail, saying that Josh had a daughter and was refusing to take responsibility. It hadn't occurred to Zane just how peculiar it was for someone to have sent that to him. He hadn't even thought too hard about why the anonymous sender would pick him as the recipient. He'd only known that it was ammunition to take down a Lowell, and that had been more than enough. "The whole point of talking to Sophie was to finally tell the world that Josh Lowell is not the savior everyone thinks he is. I even gave her personal photos to use, to show her I was a legit source. Somehow that all backfired. The DNA bombshell never made it into the anniversary article, because I picked a reporter with scruples. Now everyone seems to adore him even more than before. Just in time for him to fall in love with a beautiful woman, decide to get married and conveniently step away from Black Crescent, which is the main reason to hate him. He's getting off without a scratch, just like his dad."

Scott shook his head, the corner of his mouth turned up in a pitying smirk. "Maybe you do need a break. Get away."

"Or move."

Scott set his elbow on the table, pointing at Zane with his beer bottle. "You cannot move. I need you."

"You're drunk."

"Half a beer in? I don't think so. It's the truth. You're like a brother to me. And honestly, I think you need me. Who else is going to listen to you bitch about this?"

Scott wasn't wrong. He grounded Zane and helped him stay away from his inevitable downward spiral. "Okay. So where do I go? I need a beach, preferably with lots of women."

"It does not surprise me that you would say that."

Zane let a quiet laugh leave his lips. Yes, he had been with a lot of women over the years. That was his escape. No strings attached, no messy feelings getting in the way. In high school, it had been to numb the effects of his fall from grace. The poor former rich kid proved an easy target for other guys, but the girls didn't see it that way. His money and status might have been gone, but the body he'd spent hours working on in the gym and his face were still enough to turn a few heads. So he'd taken what he could get.

"If it's the beach you want," Scott said, "you should go down to the Bahamas. My aunt and uncle's resort off the coast of Eleuthera. I can hook you up."

Scott and Zane had talked many times about making that trip. Scott's mom was Bahamian, but had moved to the US permanently after attending college stateside and meeting Scott's dad. "Yes. Dudes' trip. We've talked about it a hundred times. It's perfect."

"Sorry, man. You're on your own. Brittney just got a promotion at work, and her schedule is crazy. It's June, so the kids are out of school. I can't just take off. Plus, if you're picking up women, I think we can both agree that my days of being your wingman are over."

Zane didn't let the disappointment get to him too much. Everything was a downer of one sort or another. He was used to it. "Okay. I guess I'm flying solo. Can you text me the info? I'll call first thing tomorrow morning."

Scott shook his head. "Just give me the dates and I'll take care of it. It's on me."

"I do not need your charity. This isn't high school."

"Will you just shut up and let me do something nice for you? Plus, I gotta keep you happy. I would be ridiculously bummed out if you moved out of Falling Brook."

Zane glanced over at Scott. He didn't know what he would do without him. He was the thing tethering him to earth. Keeping him from going off the deep end. "I'm not leaving. I might desperately need a few days on that beach to clear my head, but I'm not going anywhere." He knocked back the last of his beer. "I have to at least stick around long enough to avenge this loss."

"Black Crescent?" Scott asked.

"No. Tonight's game."

When Allison Randall saw her ex-boyfriend's name on the caller ID, she flipped off her phone. Juvenile, but incredibly satisfying.

"Let me guess. Neil?" Allison's best friend and business partner, Kianna Lewis, was perched in a chair opposite Allison's desk, flicking a pen back and forth between her thumb and forefinger. They'd been discussing the state of their corporate recruiting business, which frankly, wasn't that great.

"I really don't want to talk to him. Ever."

"Aren't the movers at his house right now? What if there's a problem?"

Kianna was so levelheaded. Allison needed that. She could get tunnel vision. And a little spiteful.

"You're right. I'm just ready for one of these conversations to be our last." Allison plucked her phone from her desk and spun her chair around to peer out the window of her office, which overlooked nothing more scenic than a sea of expensive cars in a parking lot. Such was LA—asphalt and BMWs. "What's wrong now?" she asked Neil.

"You could have hired a normal moving company, Allison. Hunks with Trucks? Seriously?" Her ex-boyfriend was not taking her departure from his life well. That was perfectly okay with her.

Allison snickered under her breath. Neil was in ridiculously good shape, and he loved to flaunt it. He took any excuse to whip off his shirt in public. Allison had figured he might as well spend the afternoon with a bunch of guys who were even more buff and cut than him. Served him right for cheating on her. "They hire college students, Neil. These guys need the work. For tuition and books. Just forget the name, okay?"

"That's a little difficult when their ten-foot-high logo is emblazoned on the truck outside my house. The neighbors can all see it."

What a drama queen. She should have known better than to date a movie producer. "Sounds like good marketing on their part."

"There's a crowd gathering. A bunch of women from my street are outside taking selfies with these guys."

This had gone far better than Allison could have anticipated. She nearly wished she'd been there to witness it, except that would have meant seeing Neil, and she couldn't guarantee she wouldn't strangle him. "If you hadn't cheated on me, you wouldn't have to suffer this supposed embarrassment."

"I made a mistake, okay? It happens. You need to get off that high horse of yours. Not everyone can be perfect like you."

She choked back a grumble. "Not cheating does not make me perfect. It makes me a decent human being, which is more than I can say for you."

"I've told you one hundred times that she meant nothing to me. It was just a few months of hookups. I was stupid for doing it, and I'm sorry."

Allison clamped her eyes shut. She was not going to let him manipulate her anymore. "I'm done with this conversation, Neil. Unless there's a real problem you need me to address, I'm going to hang up now."

"I want my key back, Alli."

"Change the locks. And don't call me Alli." She hit the red button on the screen and tossed her phone onto a pile of papers on her desk. The desire to scream was so intense she dug her fingernails into her palms.

"You okay?" Kianna asked, arching her perfectly groomed eyebrows.

"I'm fine." Allison was a firm believer in fake it 'til you make it. She would keep saying she was fine until she was actually fine. Still, the Neil situation had her shaken. How had she not seen that Neil was an arrogant jerk? How had she managed to miss the signs? As an executive recruiter, it was Allison's job to read people, but she'd clearly been all wrong about Neil.

"It's okay to have a human moment. Your boyfriend cheated on you. No one would blame you for crying or throwing things."

No, no one would fault her, but Allison refused to let this drag her down. Neil would move on with his life in his perfect house, with his suspiciously white teeth and 3 percent body fat. Allison was not going to let him be the only one to find happiness. "I'm fine. Let's get back to work. We need to finish this up so I can head over to my new place and meet the movers."

"Okay. If that's what you want." Kianna launched into a summary of their bottom line. It didn't take long. The upshot was too many expenses, not enough income. "All of this makes the Black Crescent account that much more important. If we nail this first assignment for them, we should be able to go on retainer. That will put us safely in the black."

Having a new client in her hometown of Falling Brook, New Jersey, was a real boon. Allison had pulled in a favor to make it happen, but she was sure it could translate into big things. "We can do it. I can do it. I will knock their socks off. I promise." The best part was that it would not only bring in money, she could see her brother, Scott. Allison had been there for his birthday last month, but she always looked forward to their time together.

"How soon are you planning to go out there and meet with them?"

Allison flipped through her calendar. "I haven't booked my travel yet, but I'm thinking next week. My plan is to walk into that meeting with the three amazing candidates we've been talking to for the position."

"Can I make a suggestion?"

"You think I should go sooner?"

"I think you should *leave* sooner, as in go somewhere for a few days. Relax. Unwind. Meet a hot guy and let him rock your world. Get Neil out of your system."

"But we have so much work to do."

"And we need you on top of your game when you meet with Black Crescent. You're wound way too tight right now."

Allison had to laugh. "Have you been talking to my mom?"

"Please tell me your mom didn't tell you to hook up with some guy."

"She didn't. But she did tell my aunt Angelique about Neil, and Angelique called last night begging me to come and stay with her and my uncle for a few days at their resort in the Bahamas. Bad news travels fast among the women in my family." Allison was incredibly close to her mom, so much so that she felt suffocated sometimes. So of course, they'd had many phone conversations about the Neil situation, and it was only a matter of time before her aunt found out.

"That sounds perfect. I say you do it. As long as there are men available, of course." Kianna got up from her chair, gathered her notes in her arms and headed for the door.

"A man is the last thing I need."

Kianna turned and cast Allison a stern look. "I'm not talking marriage. I'm talking sex. A few mind-blowing orgasms and Neil will be a distant memory."

"I'm not much for random hookups. I'm not even sure I can do that."

"Have you looked at yourself? Any sane guy would be psyched to take you to bed." Kianna turned on her heel and headed down the hall.

Allison wasn't sure about that, but maybe it was time to do something nice for herself—book a bungalow on the beach and fall asleep in the sun with a good book. She fumbled for her phone and dialed the number for her aunt.

"Tell me you're on the plane," Angelique said when she answered.

Allison smiled. She couldn't help it. She loved her entire family deeply. "Not yet."

"But you're coming?"

"As long as you have room for me."

"I have one bungalow open, so we have room.

It's all yours. I hope it's okay if I put you next to one of your brother's friends, though. Zane Patterson?"

That name started a long-forgotten hum in Allison's body. Zane was the guy Allison had crushed on for every waking minute of her adolescence. "He's not coming with Scott, is he?"

"Oh, no. By himself. Just for a few days. He gets here tomorrow."

Allison's heart was jackhammering in her chest. Visions of unbelievably sexy Zane rushed into her consciousness—thick dark hair with a hint of curl, piercing blue eyes that made her melt and a long, lean body she'd wanted to touch forever. She had a good dozen or so Zane fantasies she'd concocted over the years. Why had she never thought up the one where they both ended up on a secluded Bahamian island at the same time? "Oh. Funny. I was thinking I'd fly in tomorrow, too."

"Do you know him?"

"I do. He's a great guy. It's always nice to see him." Allison couldn't ignore the way her voice had suddenly pitched to a higher octave. "Nice to see him" didn't begin to cover it.

But there'd always been a massive obstacle with Zane—Scott. The only time she'd had any real physical contact with Zane was three weeks ago, when they were at her brother's house for his birthday dinner. This was right after Allison had first found out Neil was cheating. Feeling hurt, reckless and pleasantly tipsy, she'd spent most of the evening testing the waters of flirtation with Zane. She knocked her knee into his under the table, brushed his hand with her fingertips when reaching for the butter and made a point of making eye contact when she laughed at his jokes. There was a palpable connection between them, a very real spark, and she could only play with fire for so long before jumping in headfirst. So as soon as Scott and his wife left the table to put their kids to bed, Allison had grabbed her chance. She gripped Zane's muscled forearm, leaned in and kissed him. For a blissful instant, Zane was into it.

So into it.

He'd cupped her jaw with his hand like he was drinking her in. The years of wanting him day after day had been building for that moment, and she was overwhelmed by a deluge of heat and a rush of something she hadn't experienced in too long—pure hope. She arched into him, and he followed her cue, wrapping his arm around her and pressing his chest against hers. It was really happening, and her mind had leaped ahead to what came next…a quick escape, a race back to his place, clothes coming off before they were even inside, lips and hands exploring the landscape of each other's bodies until they were both exhausted. It was going to happen. Finally.

Then he froze. And everything else became a blur. He pushed her away, ashamed to look her in the eye. He blurted something about betraying Scott.

He said he was sorry. He shook his head and muttered that it had been a mistake. He pushed back from the table and rushed out the door, leaving Allison shell-shocked. How could she have been so close and have it all taken away? It felt like a cruel joke life was playing on her. It hurt like hell.

For weeks, that painful scene played in her head. But once she got beyond the hurt, she realized that the real problem had been Scott. If they'd been truly alone that night, her fantasies would've come true. She and Zane would've been naked and sweaty in no time.

But hopefully, Zane wouldn't be so worried about her hyperprotective brother if he was a thousand miles away. With close proximity to Zane and some privacy, she could finally go for what she'd always wanted—a night of pure abandon with Zane. She knew better than to hope for more than that. He was the ultimate ladies' man, and she was okay with that. He was who he was, and she still wanted him more than any man she'd ever laid eyes on. If she played her cards right, she'd at least get to fulfill this fantasy, even if it was only a onetime thing.

"Do you want me to tell him you're coming?"

If Allison had been talking to Kianna, she might have made a joke about orgasms, but that was not appropriate with her aunt. "No. Don't. I'll surprise him."

"I'm so happy you're coming to stay, Alli. It's been too long."

"I'm excited to spend some time unwinding."

"Text me your flight details. I'll have someone pick you up at the marina."

"Sounds perfect. See you tomorrow."

Allison gathered her things, closed up her office, said goodbye to Kianna and hurried out to the parking lot, feeling a new purpose in every step. She hopped into her Mercedes, cranked the stereo and headed toward her new apartment, where the guys from Hunks with Trucks would soon be waiting to move her into her new place. She wasn't even going to bother to unpack. She was going to let them in to do their work while she turned around to go shopping for a hat, a sarong and the skimpiest bikini she could find. Then she was going to get a good night's beauty sleep and get her butt on a plane tomorrow morning.

Next stop, paradise. Next stop, Zane.

Two

The flight from Miami to Eleuthera Island was not for the faint of heart. Scott's aunt and uncle Angelique and Hubert had booked a charter for Zane on the tiniest of Learjets. Still, Zane loved the freedom of hanging by an invisible thread over the jaw-dropping blue of the Atlantic.

Zane's pulse skipped a beat as the aircraft floated down to the tiny landing strip and bounced its way to an abrupt stop. Another five hundred yards and they would've been in the ocean. Engines whirring, the plane taxied around to a modest outbuilding—yellow with a rust-red roof. The crew quickly opened the cabin door, and Zane whipped off his seat belt, sucking in his first sweet breath of Bahamian air. Sunglasses on, he surveyed the landscape from his vantage point at the top of the plane stairs. Palm trees rustled in the wind, and gauzy white clouds rolled across the seemingly endless stretch of azure sky. This was exactly what he'd needed. He knew it already.

A driver from Rose Cove, the boutique resort owned by Scott's aunt and uncle, met him outside the airport building, and after a quick zip through customs, Zane was on his way to the marina in a golf cart. From there, a speedboat captain named Marcus took Zane for the two-mile trip to Rose Cove Island, off the southernmost tip of Eleuthera. The water was tranquil and clear, the wind buzzing through Zane's ears as the boat sliced through the water and the sun blanketed him in warmth. He pulled his phone out of his pocket and powered it down. He had zero plans to look at it while he was in paradise. He not only needed to unwind, he wanted to disappear. Falling Brook, the Lowell family and Black Crescent weren't even a distant thought—they'd evaporated from his mind.

Pulling up to the dock at Rose Cove, Zane was struck by the beauty of the pink sand beaches from which the tiny private island got its name. Marcus directed him down a crushed-seashell path through a tropical forest so shaded by palm trees that it was a good ten degrees cooler. Colorful birds chirped and flitted from tree to tree, while the occasional lizard skittered across the sandy ground to hide behind a rock. He eventually reached a clearing with a white single-story building of colonial architecture, with a porch that wrapped around the entire structure. Inside, Zane finally got to meet Scott's aunt Angelique.

"Welcome to Rose Cove!" she exclaimed, rushing out from behind the check-in desk, wearing a beautiful turquoise sundress, flat sandals and her braided hair pulled up in a twist. Despite her enthusiasm, Angelique's peaceful voice suggested that she lived her life at a pace far different from the rest of the world's. "My nephew has told me so much about you." She gave him a hug, showing the same warmth Zane had found in Scott's entire family. He already felt at home here. He wasn't sure he ever wanted to leave.

"You can't believe everything Scott says," Zane joked.

Angelique smiled wide. "He had nothing but great things to say." She bustled back behind the counter and unfolded what appeared to be a map. "Here's all you need to know about the island. This is the main building, where my husband, Hubert, and I live." She circled a picture of the building where they were. "The ten cottages spoke out from here and are a good distance from each other for privacy. You're in cottage number eight. You have a quiet stretch of beach, a hammock and a private plunge pool. There's a beautiful king-size bed, a luxury bath and a fully stocked kitchen. Or our staff will bring you breakfast, lunch and dinner every day. Simply fill out the card waiting for you in your room. Until then, I invite you to relax and enjoy the island. Perhaps say hello to your neighbor in cottage nine. She's been waiting for you to arrive."

"A neighbor?" *A she, no less?* Perhaps this was Zane's lucky day, although there was a part of him that knew his tendency to get lost in women was not his best trait. Really, he should be focusing on fishing and swimming while detoxing from social media and the internet.

"My niece, Allison. She arrived a few hours ago."

Zane's jaw dropped so far he had to make a conscious decision to close his mouth. He was flabbergasted. What were the chances that he and Allison would end up on the island at the same time? "Allison is here. On this island. Right now."

"Is there a problem?"

He shook his head so fast he nearly lost his sunglasses, which were resting on top of his head. "Absolutely not. I love Allison. I'm just surprised. I'll have to stop over and say hi." He hadn't seen Allison much in the years since he graduated from high school. He'd gone to college in North Carolina on a basketball scholarship, and when he returned to Falling Brook after four years, she was off to school in Los Angeles, where she stayed to start a business. She returned every Christmas, but Zane always seemed to be visiting his mom in Boston at the same time.

But three weeks ago Scott's wife, Brittney, invited both Allison and Zane to a surprise birthday dinner she was having for Scott. Allison flew in for the weekend. The instant Zane saw her, he knew exactly how good the years had been to Allison—almost too good. She'd taken a straight line from cute to drop-dead gorgeous. Her long and wavy black hair was pulled back in a ponytail, showing off the incredible depth and warmth of her brown eyes. The chemistry of the entire room shifted when she smiled or laughed. He'd always found her interesting and a bit otherworldly, with a style and vibe all her own, but that night he was transfixed.

She'd surprised him many times when they were younger, like the day she got her nose pierced, but she'd flat-out shocked him that night at Scott's house. She kissed him—soft and sensuous and so packed with sexy intent that he'd felt the earth shift beneath him. He was so conditioned to think of Allison only as his best friend's little sister that he'd been wholly unprepared for Allison, the fully formed woman. And with Scott in the other room, a man to whom there would be no explaining, Zane had done the unthinkable that night. He'd pushed beautiful, beguiling Allison away.

"Well, she has the cottage next to yours, so I'm sure you'll see her," Angelique said.

Now Zane was wondering how in the hell he was going to navigate these difficult waters. He didn't want to relive the awkward aftermath of that kiss. Their conversation from that night was permanently emblazoned on his psyche.

This is wrong, Allison. Your brother.

Don't talk about Scott.

But he's right in the other room. He will never forgive me.

Women had been Zane's escape many times, but not like that. Never before had he risked one of the most important things in his life for a kiss.

It had been such a blur, Zane had left without saying so much as goodbye to Scott, asking Allison to tell him that he had a headache. She told him he was getting freaked out for nothing, but Zane knew his weakness when it came to women, and Allison was the one woman he absolutely could never have.

"Mr. Patterson? Are you sure everything is okay? Scott mentioned that you've been under a lot of stress." Angelique looked at him quizzically, knocking her head to one side.

"Oh, yes. Sorry." He shook his head in an effort to get it straight. He needed to get a grip. He and Allison had shared a kiss. It was no big deal. Scott would never know about it, and it would never happen again—end of story.

"Is there anything else you need?"

"My room key, I guess."

"There are no keys on Rose Cove. You will enjoy more seclusion and privacy than you ever imagined.

But I'm happy to have someone show you to your cottage."

Zane picked up the map from the registration counter. "Not necessary. I think I've got it from here."

"You can't get too lost. Just stop when you reach the ocean." Angelique winked and grinned, then waved goodbye.

Zane followed the path and the small wood signs to cottages eight and nine. As he walked under the canopy of trees, he had to remind himself that Allison was not fair game. He would be friendly and cordial. He might even spend a small bit of time with her while they were both there, but there would be no replay of that kiss. Scott was too important to him. He would not betray the bro code. Never.

Ahead, Zane could see the water and two cottages set several hundred yards away from each other, one a shade of sky blue and the other pure turquoise, each with painted white trim and a bright red roof. All around them, the powdery pink sand was a bright and summery accent, while the sun glinted off the calm crystalline sea. It could not have been a more stunning setting, and despite his worries over how he would handle the situation with Allison, Zane could feel himself unwinding, his spine loosening and his shoulders relaxing.

He opened the door to his cottage and stepped inside, his eyes immediately drawn to the stunning vista of ocean at the far end of the house. He set down the map and strolled through the open living room, which had a vaulted wood-beamed ceiling and entire wall of windows, all open and letting in the sea breezes. At center was a set of oversize French doors, which led out to Zane's patio, covered in terracotta tile with an arbor above it for shade. Beyond that was his private plunge pool, surrounded by lush tropical plantings.

Not wanting to wait another minute for his vacation to start, Zane found the bedroom, which, as advertised, had an intricately carved wood bed with another beautiful view of the sea. His suitcase had been delivered by staff, and he wasted no time getting into his swim trunks, grabbing a towel from the beautifully appointed bathroom and making one more stop in the kitchen to grab a beer. He poured it into a shatterproof tumbler, and, sunglasses on, he strolled out onto the terrace and jumped into the pool.

The water was cool and exhilarating, the perfect counterpoint to the strong Bahamian sun. He slicked his hair back from his face and swam over to the edge of the pool, folding his arms up on the edge and drinking in the beautiful ocean view. As difficult as the last few weeks had been—hell, the last several years—Zane could feel that all fading away. Scott had been so right. Maybe he just needed some time to clear his head and stop thinking about Josh Lowell and Black Crescent.

Zane dropped his chin down onto the back of his hand and something caught his eye. More specifically, someone—a woman sauntering down to the water in front of the other cabin. *Allison.* It had to be her. She was turned away from him, but he'd have to be dead to not admire the view—her hair down the middle of her back, tawny skin set against a colorful sarong, lithe legs and bare feet. She stopped where the pink sand met the water and turned, ambling in his direction while gently swishing her feet in beautiful blue.

He wasn't sure what to do. Call out to her? Submerge himself in icy water and try to hide for the next five days? This never, ever would have been a question if she hadn't kissed him on Scott's birthday. She was permanently off-limits, fruit so forbidden that he would be blowing up his entire life if he dared to go there.

Before he had a chance to formulate any sort of plan, Allison looked up and spotted him. His heart instantly began pulsing, jumping to double time when she raised her sunglasses up onto her forehead for a moment, smiled and waved. Good God, she was unfairly beautiful. And she was coming his way. He had no means of stopping this. He had to go with it and try to have a casual conversation with the sister of his best friend.

So he did what he would have done if they'd never kissed—he waved back and called her name. "Allison!"

As Allison walked up the beach toward Zane's cottage, she could hardly believe this was really happening. How many times had she concocted some dream scenario in her head where she and Zane were alone? Too many to count. And what was unfolding before her was exactly the kind of fantasy she loved to weave—a perfect sunny day, not another human in sight, the breeze brushing her skin and the air so sweet.

Her pulse raced. Every nerve ending in her body was firing. Her breaths were deep, and yet she still felt as though she couldn't get enough oxygen. If she wasn't careful, she was going to hyperventilate or pass out. This was Zane's effect on her. It was as if the real Allison was no longer in control and some other version of her was pulling the strings. It had been like this since she was thirteen and he was sixteen.

But Zane wasn't a teenager anymore. And she wasn't, either. She was twenty-eight years old, and she knew what she wanted. She also knew that the world didn't go around handing out opportunities. Life didn't work like that. You had to take what was yours when you had the chance. And as she got closer to Zane's cottage and watched him climb out of his plunge pool, water dripping from his magnificent, lean and athletic form, she didn't even have to ask herself what her goal was—she knew it in her heart and in her gut. She wanted Zane's naked body pressed against hers. She needed his mouth on every inch of her. She had to have him, if only for a few days in paradise. Zane was not "for keeps," but he could absolutely be "for right now."

"Hey there," she said, stepping up onto his patio. She studied him as he toweled off his chest. She'd only seen him with this shirt off a few times, but his shoulders were just as amazing as she'd remembered. Firm and contoured from thousands of hours playing basketball. His chest was even more glorious, with a tiny patch of dark hair right at the center. She wanted to tangle her fingers in that hair. She wanted to kiss him there. She hungered to skim her lips over every inch of his pecs, rake her fingernails across the warm skin of his abs and tease open the drawstring of his swim trunks.

"How weird is this?" Zane rattled her back to the present with the question. In her fantasies, he would have opened with something far more seductive. Maybe something like, *Hello, beautiful. Can I help you with your sarong?* "We live on opposite ends of the country but we both end up at your aunt and uncle's resort at the same time?"

"What are the chances, huh? Small world, I suppose." She couldn't help but notice his body language—

shoulders tight and hands clutching the towel to his chest, as if he was hiding from her. This was all wrong, and she was desperate to change the dynamic. "Can I have a hug?"

"Uh, sure. Of course." He grabbed his T-shirt from one of the chaise longues by the pool and put it on. He was definitely trying to keep his distance. She might need to take things slow. She didn't want to scare him off or freak him out. The last thing her already-bruised ego needed was another interaction like the one at Scott's birthday party. She couldn't endure it if he pushed her away again. She spread out her arms and gave him the sort of embrace only friends exchange. It was quick and to the point, and not at all what she wanted. Just that one little taste of his body heat left her longing. Her chest ached for more.

"So what are you doing here?" he asked.

"I needed a break, and my aunt is always begging me to visit."

"Things stressful at work?"

She looked around for a place to sit. "Do you mind?" She gestured to one of two chaises under an umbrella.

"Yeah. Of course. Do you want a beer?"

"I'm good for now, but thanks." She did want one, but she wasn't sure it was a good idea. She needed to keep her wits about her while she was trying to suss out where his head was at. They hadn't talked once since the kiss a few weeks ago. For all she knew, he thought she was a lunatic. "I just broke up with my boyfriend. We were living together, so it was a pretty big ordeal, moving out and all of that."

Zane sat in the chair next to her and reclined, crossing his legs at the ankle. He had incredibly sexy legs, a mile long but still pure muscle, with just the right amount of dark hair. "I'm sorry to hear that. If you need a shoulder to cry on, I'm a pretty good listener. Plus, I figure I'm forever in debt to the Randall family."

"For what?"

"Where do I start? Turning around my entire life when I was at my lowest point?"

Allison waved it off. He still clung to a debt of gratitude for her family, but the truth was that Zane had given them a lot, too. He'd never been anything less than a positive presence. For Scott and Allison, who'd had a mostly stable childhood, watching Zane battle through his family's reversal of fortune had taught them a lot about humility. "Are you kidding me? My parents love you. And obviously Scott is obsessed with you." Her phone, which she had tucked into her bathing suit top, rang. Things at work were so tenuous right now that she couldn't afford to turn off her ringer, as much as she wanted uninterrupted time with Zane. "I'm sorry. I should look to see who it is." She glanced at the caller ID. It was Scott. Did he have some sort of psychic ability to interrupt her at the most inopportune time? For an instant, she considered sending the call to voice mail, but she knew that he would just keep calling her back.

"Speak of the devil," she said to Zane. "It's my brother."

"Oh. Wow."

"I know." She answered the call to speak to Scott. "Were your ears ringing? We were just talking about you."

"What the hell, Allison? You're down at Rose Cove by yourself and Zane is there, too?"

Of course he's not only calling, he's taken issue with the fact that I'm with Zane. "Yes. I'm doing this thing where you travel to a place where you don't live and you relax. It's called vacation. You should try it." She glanced over at Zane, who she hoped would at least be smiling after her wisecrack at her brother. But no. Zane's handsome face was painted with entirely too much concern. She'd seen that look before, and she didn't like it.

"Is there something funny going on between you two?" Scott asked. "Don't think I didn't notice how weird you were being at my party."

Being under Scott's thumb had grown so tiresome. In many ways, Allison felt as though she'd been born under it. "We're hanging out. He's my friend, too."

Zane cleared his throat. "Hand me the phone."

Allison shook her head and held the receiver to her chest. "No. I've got this. He's being ridiculous, and you and I are sitting by the pool, talking. He needs to get over himself." She raised the phone back to her ear. "Unless you have something nice to say to me, I'm going to say goodbye now and get back to my vacation."

"He went on this trip to hook up with women," Scott blurted. "He told me as much. And I do not want you to fall for his charms. Nothing good comes of it, and you just came off a bad breakup."

Allison grumbled under her breath. As if she needed another reminder that Zane had a zillion other women waiting in the wings. Her brother was ruining her fantasy, and she wasn't going to sit around for any more of it. "Okay. Sounds great."

"You aren't listening to me. You're just saying that so Zane won't know what I'm saying about him."

"Yep. You're right. Anything else? I need to get going."

"Are you watching the forecast? There's a system forming in the Atlantic. The weather channel says it could dip down into the Caribbean. It could be upgraded to a tropical storm by late today. It could easily become a hurricane."

Allison looked overhead. There wasn't a cloud in the sky. "You are such a weather nerd. I'm not worried about something an ocean away, okay? Plus, it's June. The hurricane season just started. I'm sure Angelique and Hubert will let us know if it's anything of concern.

Now, go back to your life so I can try to unwind. Kiss the kids for me."

"I'm calling you tomorrow. And just punch Zane if he tries anything. Or remind him I will kill him if he touches you."

Allison didn't want to tell Scott that if there was any smacking going on, it would be only of the playful variety, and only if she was very lucky. "Got it. Love you." She pushed the red button on her phone and tucked it back inside her swimsuit top. "Sorry about that. I think he's paranoid that there's something going on between us."

Zane got up from his seat and ran his hand through his hair. His forehead creases were deep with worry. "Then you need to call him back and tell him that absolutely nothing is going on. Or I'll do it. Give me your phone."

Allison sat back on the chaise and didn't bother to cover up when her sarong slipped open, revealing the full stretch of her bare leg and a good bit of her stomach, as well. She loved seeing the way Zane tried not to look…and failed. Did he want her the way she wanted him? Did he crave her touch? Her kiss? The thought of unleashing all of her pent-up desire on him, especially in paradise, where they could be blissfully alone, was so tempting it made her entire body tingle. It would be so easy to undo the knot of her cover-up and let it fall away. Give Zane an eyeful. Run her fingers along the edge of her bikini top, right where the swell of her breasts could draw the most attention. She wanted to do it so badly that her hand twitched. But she had to play this slowly. "Don't be threatened by my brother. He's just watching out for me. It's a bad habit of his. He needs to cut it out."

"You know why he's so protective of you. There's a good reason for it."

Allison did know there was a good reason, but she'd been a little girl when she got sick. She hardly remembered any of it—it was practically a lifetime ago. Most important, she was perfectly healthy now and had been cancer-free for more than twenty years. Her entire family needed to stop hovering over her like she was made of porcelain. "And because my family is always around, I think we should take this chance to hang out on our own terms. Talk. Like friends. We are friends, aren't we?"

"I don't know."

"What? You don't know if we're friends?"

He shook his head, seeming frustrated, which was not what she was going for. She wanted him relaxed. At ease. "I don't know if it's a good idea for us to spend time together."

"What are you afraid of, Zane? That I'm going to kiss you again?" She had a sliver of regret at putting things on the line like this at the outset, but perhaps it was for the best. If he was going to reject her, best to get it out of the way.

"For starters, yes."

Allison pressed her lips together tightly. She decided then and there that if any moves were going to be made, the first would have to be his. If he wanted her the way she wanted him, he was going to have to show her. She wasn't putting her heart and pride on the line a second time, especially not when he was so willing to say out loud that he was worried about what she might do. "I promise I won't kiss you, okay? Just stop acting like you're afraid of me, because I know you aren't."

"Of course I'm not afraid."

"Then prove it. Let me make you dinner."

Zane ran his tongue across his lower lip tentatively. It was one of his most adorable quirks and he always did it when he couldn't make up his mind about something. Allison didn't like that her offer required any deliberation at all, but she certainly appreciated the vision of his mouth. "Dinner? Nothing else?"

Allison closed up her sarong and rose from her seat. "Fair warning. You might go home incredibly satisfied." She patted him on the shoulder. "From my cooking. It's really good."

Three

Zane's entire body was humming when Allison left, which left his brain running at a clip to catch up. If Scott knew what was going through Zane's head right now and how that all centered on his little sister, he would end him. It wouldn't be a quick death. It would be a long, painful one, during which Scott would drive home a single point—Allison was off-limits. Always had been. Always would be.

But here on a dot of an island, more than a thousand miles away from his best friend, Zane couldn't deny his churning thoughts or the insistent pulse of electricity in his body. The second Allison's sarong fell open to reveal the tops of her luscious thighs, the soft plane of her stomach and that little spot on her hip where the tie of her bikini bottoms sat, all bets were off. Or most of them, at least. He'd withstood an unholy rush of blood to the center of his body, so fierce that it nearly knocked him off his feet. Thinking about it was only providing an opportunity to put a finer point on the things he'd wanted to do to her—drop to his knees, start at her ankle and kiss every inch of her lovely leg, moving north until he reached the bow at her hip. The only thing that would make sense if he ever got that far would be to tug at the string, quite possibly with his teeth, slowly untie it and use his mouth to leave her curling her fingers into his scalp and calling out his name.

Thoughts like that were going to ruin Zane and everything he held dear.

He stalked into his cottage and opened the fridge, if nothing but for the blast of cold air against his overheated skin. It didn't help. It somehow made everything worse—another bodily conflict to endure as the shot of coolness mixed with the balmy salt air—everything on this island felt good. Too good. He popped open another beer and took a swig, but dammit, it was only a pleasing jolt of sweet and bitter, a shock of frothy cold followed by a wave of warmth that made him pleasantly dizzy. The erection he'd tried so desperately to fight off was now at a full salute, begging for attention and hungry for release.

There was only one way to get past this, and it

didn't involve an icy shower. He couldn't wash away Allison's effect on him. He had to get past it. He stormed off to his bedroom, shucked his clothes and stretched out on the magnificent bed. The linens were smooth and impossibly soft against his skin, another pleasure he didn't relish, but this was the only way to keep himself from doing something foolish later tonight when he saw Allison. It was time to take matters—namely, his erection—into his own hands.

He didn't bother with seduction, reaching down and wrapping his fingers around his length. He closed his eyes and allowed himself the luxury of visions of Allison—glossy hair framing those deep, soulful eyes, plump lips and a smile that could turn ice to a puddle. Her shapely legs and curvy hips. Her luscious breasts. He took long strokes with his hand, imagining kissing her again, except there was no stopping this time. He started things, and she turned up the volume, their tongues winding, mouths hot and wet and hungry for more.

The tension in his body built, but coiled tighter, a push and pull he wouldn't be able to take for long. To edge himself closer, he conjured an illusion of Allison naked and the feeling of her body on top of him, holding him down with her warmth and softness. He imagined being inside her—the closeness, the heat—and her heady sweetness perfuming the air as he brought her to her peak. With that thought, the pressure was released and he arched his back, riding out the waves of pleasure. His breath hitched in a sharp inhale, then came out in a long rush of relief. He settled back on the pillow and slowly pried his eyes open, not to the sight of Allison but to the white painted ceiling and whirring fan overhead. He turned and glanced at the clock on the nightstand. He had four hours until dinner. Hopefully this solo rendezvous had prepared him. Now to shower, read a few chapters of a book, take a nap and hope that he could keep his libido in check.

Five minutes before six, Zane headed to Allison's cottage, dressed in jeans and a dress shirt with the sleeves rolled up to the elbows. He carried his flip-flops and walked barefoot through the sand, which was still warm from the day's rays. Over the water, the sun was dipping lower, painting the sky in vibrant shades of pink and orange. It was so obvious and easy to say, but Rose Cove really was paradise. He didn't want to leave anytime soon. Having distance from his past and from Joshua Lowell? Amazing. If it weren't for Scott, and Zane's company, he might never go back to Falling Brook.

He found himself taking his time as he strolled across the beach, now approaching Allison's. She had every window and door flung open, allowing him to watch her in the kitchen, milling about. He really hoped she wasn't going to put the full-court press on him tonight, and that her only intention was for the two of them to spend a few hours together. It was time to leave The Kiss where it belonged—in the past. Their circumstances did not allow for him to ever go there again. One thing he'd learned when his parents lost every penny of the family's money to Black Crescent and Joshua Lowell's father was that the sooner you learned to accept your personal situation and deal with what you had in front of you, the better.

"Knock, knock," Zane said, standing at the French doors to Allison's cottage. "I brought a bottle of wine, but I can't really take credit for it. Your aunt stocked my fridge."

Allison turned and smiled, looking fresh-faced and sun kissed, wearing a swishy black skirt and a royal blue tank top. Her feet were again bare and her hair was up in a high ponytail. There wasn't a single made-up thing about her, and that made her perfect, however much he wished he hadn't noticed. *She's your best friend's little sister. Don't be an idiot.* It was his new mantra. He committed himself to repeating it over and over until it became part of his psyche.

"I'm glad you came." She took the wine from him and carried it straight to the kitchen counter. No kiss on the cheek hello. No hug.

Zane was relieved, even if there was something in his body that was registering as disappointment. "Well, you know, I had so many invitations, I wasn't sure what to do." He took a seat at the kitchen island, with a view of the cooktop, where something delicious-smelling was simmering away.

Allison laughed, then handed him the corkscrew. "Here. Make yourself useful."

"Yes, ma'am." He got up and opened the bottle, then took the liberty of finding the wineglasses, which was easily done since this kitchen had the exact layout of his own. "To friends." He offered her a glass and held up his own for the toast.

"Yes. To friends." She took a sip, hardly looking at him at all.

He wondered if he'd been too standoffish earlier. He only wanted to keep things in a place where nobody got hurt. He didn't want to lose *all* of the warmth between them. Just some of it. Keep things friendly, but not too friendly. "Have you seen any of the other guests on the island at all?" he asked.

She shook her head and lifted the lid off a pot. "I haven't. Angelique stopped by and told me that a few people canceled their reservations because there's talk of a hurricane."

"That's what you were talking about with Scott, isn't it?" This didn't sit well with Zane. It would be just his luck that the weather would go bad and ruin his idyllic vacation. Worse than that, they were sitting ducks if a bad storm came through.

"Don't worry. Both Angelique and Hubert said this happens all the time. The forecasts are often wildly inaccurate, and the models have the storm going any number of directions." Allison gestured outside with a nod. "Look at that sunset. There's no way a storm is coming."

He stole a glance, even though he'd been admiring it minutes earlier. "You're probably right."

"You need to relax, Zane. The whole point of being here is to unwind. Dinner is just about ready."

Zane had thought he was relaxed. Apparently not. "What are we having?"

"A conch ceviche with lime and fresh chilies to start, then baked crab with rice and pigeon peas. All my mom's family recipes."

"That's why it smells so amazing. It makes me think of your mom and being at your house."

"Of course. She must have made this for you one of the times you stayed with us." Allison spooned the ceviche into two small dishes and sprinkled fresh herbs on top.

"That seems like forever ago." Being with Allison while memories of time with her family surfaced had Zane wedged between nostalgia and the pain of that period of his life. It was about so much more than the financial struggle. The real misery had come from watching his parents' marriage fall apart before his very eyes. Allison was a reminder of both things he cherished and things he wished had never happened, which he knew was part of the reason every sense was heightened around her. "You were just a girl then. How old were you when we met? Thirteen?"

She cast him a disapproving look. "I'm all for memory lane, but can we not talk about me as an awkward teenager?"

"Why? You were the coolest kid I ever met. You had the best taste in music. You were always reading all of these books I'd never heard of. You totally had your own fashion sense. You'd wear those flowery dresses and black Doc Martens boots. Or T-shirts with bands I'd never heard of."

Allison blushed and tried to hide a smile. "Will you please shut up? It's embarrassing."

Zane couldn't help but love that they had this history and that he could have playfully tease her because of it. She'd always had a tough outer shell, carrying herself with an air of disaffection. She wanted the world to think that she didn't care what anyone thought of her, but Zane had long suspected that wasn't quite the case. "It's the truth. That was the first thing that struck me about you. You always had an amazing sense of self. I'm not sure I ever did."

"I think you've always known exactly who you are. The problem is that you weren't always happy about it."

For a moment, the air in the room seemed to stand still. Was that his problem? Or was it that the wounds inflicted by the Lowell family had been so slow to heal? "Well, if that's the case, it's only because I'm pretty easy to figure out. Feed me and I'm happy."

He smiled, hoping to lighten the mood. He'd never intended to steer them down such a serious path.

"Then I'm your girl." She held up the two dishes of ceviche.

Zane swallowed hard, and not because the food was so mouthwatering. He was reading too much into everything Allison did and said. And it was going to be his undoing if he wasn't careful. Again, he reminded himself to relax. He was more than capable of enjoying a beautiful home-cooked meal with an old friend. "Should we eat out on the patio?"

"Whatever and wherever you want."

Allison had to hand it to herself—dinner was incredible. Her mom and Aunt Angelique would be proud.

Zane sat back in one of the lounge chairs out on the patio, rubbing his belly and gazing up at the stars. "That was unbelievable. I don't think I'm going to need to eat again anytime soon."

"You went back for seconds. I'm impressed."

He turned and smiled at her, and, even in the darkness, with only the faint light from inside the house, she was struck by just how damn handsome he was—kissable lips, stormy eyes and the smile of a heartbreaker. The sight of him made her breath catch in her throat in a painfully familiar way. It was exactly like every other time she'd tormented herself with the conscious thought of how perfect he was.

"Like I said, feed me and I'm happy. You fed me so well, I'd have to say I'm euphoric."

It was reassuring to know she could do this much right, but this entire evening had too many echoes of the past—the friendship was there between them, but she wanted more. She would always want more. The itch to be with him would never go away unless she had the chance to scratch it. "Any interest in working off that meal tomorrow?" She knew that there was a little too much innuendo in the wording of her question, but it was meant to be a test.

"What'd you have in mind?" He returned his sights to the night sky, not taking the chance to flirt with her.

Any other woman might be deterred or discouraged, but Allison hadn't come this close to give up now. She would forge ahead with her suggestion and keep the ball in his court. "Snorkeling. If we hike around to the north side of the island, the water and fish are unbelievable. If we're lucky, we'll see sea turtles, too. We can swim out right from the beach."

He was doing that thing with his tongue and his lower lip again, driving her crazy in the process. "Yeah. Cool. That sounds fun. What time?"

Allison wanted to spend the entire day with him, and the sun would be too strong by midday to spend too much time in the water. "Morning is best if you can haul your butt out of bed. Nine o'clock?" Just then, her phone rang. Out of habit, she'd brought it with her out onto the patio. She glanced at the caller ID and knew she had to take it. She didn't want to interrupt her evening with Zane, but this was one of her Black Crescent candidates, someone she'd been trading phone calls with for a few days. "I'm so sorry. I need to get this. You can go if you want to. I'll see you tomorrow morning." She scrambled up out of her seat and pressed the button to answer the call. "Hello? Ryan?"

"Hi, Ms. Randall. I'm so glad I reached you," Ryan Hathaway answered.

"Me, too. I've been waiting to talk to you." Allison shuffled off into the house, but something stopped her from going too far—Zane's hand on her bare shoulder. She froze, but only because that one touch was making her head swim. The power he had over her was immense. If anything ever did happen between them, she might burst into flames.

"Hey. I thought we were having a nice night." Zane glanced at the phone. "Now I feel like you're blowing me off for someone else."

Allison raised the receiver back to her ear. "Ryan, can you hold on for one minute? I need to take care of something."

"Sure thing," Ryan replied.

"Thank you. I promise it'll only be a minute." She pressed the mute button on the screen. "We were having a nice night, but all good things must come to an end, right?" She didn't want to brush off Zane, but this call was incredibly important. Not just for her, either. Kianna was counting on her.

"Well, yeah, but you're also the one who was talking a big game to your brother about relaxing and unwinding while you're here. I turned off my phone completely. It's back at my place."

"This is work, okay?" The realization hit her hard. It wasn't merely work. This was Black Crescent, and Zane might never forgive her if he found out she was working for them. The decision to pursue business with BC had been easy enough to rationalize when Zane was living on the opposite side of the country. After all, it had been fifteen years since Vernon Lowell took off with all that money, and the current powers that be at BC were not like him. But now that she and Zane were inches away from each other, and her mind had been flooded with memories since seeing him, she understood just how betrayed he might feel if he discovered the truth.

"It's nine thirty at night."

"I know. My work calls happen at odd times sometimes. I'm sorry, but I really need to take this. So you can either stay or go, but I need a few minutes."

Zane nodded, but seemed entirely suspicious. "Cool. I'll clean the kitchen while you talk."

Dammit. Allison knew there was no way she could talk to Ryan with Zane in the same room, and she ran the risk of him joining her if she went back out to the patio. "Great. I'll take the call in my bedroom." Without further explanation, she ducked into her bedroom and closed the door. "Ryan. I'm so sorry."

"No problem, Ms. Randall."

"Please. Call me Allison."

"Okay, Allison. I've rearranged my schedule so I can be back in Falling Brook for the interview next week. I'll get in the night before."

Allison loved how prepared and thorough Ryan was. "Perfect. And you're sure you're okay with the idea of working for this company in particular?" She highly doubted that Zane might be listening at her door, but she still hoped hard that he wasn't. It hadn't been her intention to hurt Zane when she'd taken the BC gig. She was trying to save her company.

"I am. I know the history. It's pretty crazy all of the stuff that happened with the Lowell family, and of course I hate that Vernon Lowell ruined so many families. But maybe that's why they need somebody like me at the helm."

"That's a great attitude to have. They've really put that past behind them and are focused on the future. This job is the chance of a lifetime. No one ever imagined the CEO position could go to someone outside the family." Allison sucked in a deep breath, amazed she'd managed to keep herself from uttering the name Joshua Lowell.

"I agree. It's an excellent opportunity. I'm excited

to interview and I'm excited to finally meet you in person, too."

"Sounds great. I'm in the Bahamas right now visiting family, but I'll see you in Falling Brook next week. Good night, Ryan."

"Have a wonderful vacation. Good night."

Allison ended the call and for a moment, stared at the back of her bedroom door. She felt as though she were teetering on the edge of a cliff. The Black Crescent account was crucial to the success of her company, and she'd promised Kianna she would nail this first assignment BC had given them. But she also knew firsthand the damage inflicted by BC, and exactly how Zane would feel if and when he found out that she was working for them. This absolutely put a wrench in her romantic hopes, but she reminded herself that Zane would never be a long-term thing. He wanted the physical parts and none of the emotional entanglements. Yes, she was risking their friendship, but, in her experience, those things could be mended. If needed, she could get Scott to talk Zane off the ledge, tell him that the Black Crescent thing was just business. Surely a friend could understand that.

She opened her door and walked back into the main room. Zane was drying one of the hand-painted platters she'd used. "Hey. I'm so sorry."

"Don't apologize. I shouldn't have given you a hard time. You have things you have to do. I get it."

"Thank you. I appreciate that."

Zane set down the clean dish and leaned against the kitchen counter. "Nice guy?"

"What?"

"The guy you were talking to. You seemed pretty chummy. I thought it was just you and your partner in that office."

For a moment, Allison struggled to figure out what he was asking, but then she realized there was the slightest chance that Zane was jealous. That was so incongruous with his personality that it didn't really compute. He could have any woman he wanted. And he'd pushed her away the one time they'd kissed. "Great guy, actually. Supersmart. Handsome, too."

"Yeah? Could there be something brewing between you two?"

He might not be jealous, but he was curious, which made her both nervous and a bit exhilarated. "I hate to disappoint you, but no. He's a recruit. Nothing else."

Zane nodded. "Oh. Okay."

She scanned his face, and he returned the look. Good God, she had the most urgent desire to show him the reason why a guy like Ryan Hathaway was not what she wanted. If only she could press Zane against that kitchen counter and kiss him into oblivion, thread her hands into his hair and show him just how badly she longed for him. She wanted to tell him everything—that she'd fantasized about him hundreds of times, how she needed to finally get him out of her system. Being this close to him and knowing she couldn't do any of that was testing what little resolve she had left. But she had to hold strong. She would not make the first move.

"I should probably get going," Zane said, finally breaking their eye contact. "Get out of your hair."

"You aren't in my hair, Zane. This is fun. I could talk to you all night." She did her best to hide the soft rumble in her voice, the way she secretly wanted to beckon him to her bedroom with her tone.

"I need to get a good night's sleep if we're going to go snorkeling tomorrow."

Tomorrow. Allison could wait until then. Tomorrow was another chance to show Zane that she was a woman. He'd been with so many over the years, why not her? Why couldn't she have at least one taste of him? "Right. Snorkeling."

He pushed off from the kitchen counter and walked to the door leading out to her patio. Allison followed, tormented and enticed by everything about him. "Thanks for dinner. It was amazing." He ran his hands through his thick hair, seeming at least a little conflicted. She took solace in that. She was at war with herself, too.

"You're more than welcome."

He leaned in and pecked her on the cheek. It happened so fast, she had no time to grip his arms or pull him closer or even simply wish for a real kiss.

It only left her once again hungry for everything she couldn't have.

"See you tomorrow morning."

"Yep. Got it." She watched as he disappeared down the beach, into the darkness. It hurt to see him go without leaving her more, but she'd felt this way about Zane forever. The yearning might never go away. It might always be an unanswered question. Still, she really wished he would finally get up enough nerve to be the one to break their never-ending standoff. Her heart couldn't take much more.

Four

Zane woke with the sun and too many thoughts rolling around in his head. He was excited by the prospect of spending the day with Allison. Snorkeling with a friend sounded fun, and "fun" was something he so rarely had. But last night had been a close call from his side of things. He'd wanted to kiss Allison so badly that he'd volunteered to clean her kitchen— not his favorite activity.

What was keeping him from going for what he wanted? He'd never felt shy about it in the past. His greatest fear was Scott finding out, even though in all likelihood, Zane and Allison could do whatever they wanted without fear of repercussions. But guilt would crush him alive. Betrayal was at the top of Zane's to-not-do list. He needed trust in his life. He'd learned that the hard way when he was a teenager and his life fell apart. Everything he'd ever counted on—the stability of his family and, more important, his parents' marriage—was upended. He realized then just how badly he needed to be able to trust in something or someone. But that was a two-way street—if he couldn't be trustworthy in return, what was he doing with his life? Giving in to his desire for Allison would give Scott every reason in the world to feel betrayed. He'd never breached their friendship like that and he didn't want to start now.

He was assuming a lot, though. Just because Allison had once kissed him didn't mean she still wanted that from him. She'd taken that phone call last night and seemed eager to distance herself. She'd said it was about work, but Zane wasn't convinced. Why duck into the other room and close the door behind her? She was an executive recruiter, not an undercover FBI agent. She obviously had some new guy after her, which should come as absolutely no surprise. Or perhaps she was doing the pursuing. He could imagine that, too.

Get a grip, Zane. Get a damn grip. Allison was his friend. Last night, they'd had a friendly dinner. Today, they were going on an adventure. This was meant to be fun. It was meant to be platonic. Nothing more.

He slathered on sunscreen, got dressed in his swim trunks and headed over to Allison's cottage. She was hanging out on her patio, again on the phone. He waved at her and, although she returned the gesture, she quickly shot up out of her chaise, plugging a finger in her free ear and hustling back into the house. Perhaps it was work again. He hadn't realized Allison was quite so driven, but it would certainly be in line with her personality. Then again, there was the chance that it was a guy. Definitely a plausible explanation. He hung out next to her pool while she finished her call, taking deep breaths and admiring the gentle lap of the water on the sand.

"Hey. Sorry," Allison said, reappearing from inside the house. She was wearing her sarong again and through the thin fabric, it was apparent she was wearing that same maddening bikini.

He prayed for strength. So much strength. "Everything okay? It wasn't Scott giving you a hard time again, was it?"

She unleashed her electric smile, which calmed him, but sent a noticeable thrill through him, as well. "No. Although, he did call again last night. He keeps telling me to watch the forecast. And to watch out for you."

Zane directed his sights skyward. "It's another beautiful day in paradise. And I think we demonstrated last night that there's no need to worry about anything else."

She nodded. "Right? He needs to get a hobby."

"I could call him and tell him to get to work, but I promised myself I wouldn't turn on my phone once while I'm here." Zane deliberately delivered a pointed glance. "Maybe you should try the same thing."

She looked at her phone and hesitated. "You know, I think that's a great idea. I will do that. I've already talked to my partner today, and honestly, I think it'll be good for Scott to not be able to reach either of us for a few days. Let him wonder what's going on." She bounced her eyebrows playfully.

Zane felt a distinct tug from his stomach. He didn't want Scott worrying, but there was likely no avoiding that, with or without phone contact with his sister. "We ready to head out?"

"Yes. My uncle had someone drop off the snorkel gear for us about an hour ago." She grabbed two mesh drawstring bags that were sitting on the patio tile next to the French doors. "I just need help getting sunscreen on my back before we get in the water. And I'm guessing you do, too."

Indeed, that had been the one place Zane hadn't been able to reach on his own. He considered accepting the reality of a sunburn, but skin cancer was no joke. "Yep."

He followed Allison into her cottage, where she had a bottle of SPF 50 on the kitchen counter. "I'll do you first. Turn around."

Zane swallowed hard at the notion of either of them *doing* the other, but followed Allison's directive. He heard the squishy sounds as she rubbed the lotion between her hands, and even though he knew it was coming, he winced when she touched him.

"Still cold?" she asked as she began to spread the silky liquid over his back and shoulders.

"No. No. It feels great." He closed his eyes to attempt to ward off how damn good it felt to have her touch him. This was what he'd wanted, if only for an instant, that night that she'd kissed him. They'd been fully clothed then. Not now. Instead, they not only had too much bare skin between them, they also had privacy, solitude and an entire sunny day stretching out in front of them. He tried to quiet his mind, but that only put the physical sensations at center stage. Her hands were pure magic as she worked the lotion into his shoulders, then down his spine until she reached his waist. He heard her pour more into her hands, then she swiped the velvety cream in circles at the small of his back.

"You're good to go," she said, handing him the bottle. "Now me."

He turned, only to see that she'd taken off her sarong and tossed it aside. And now he was confronted with her in that tiny black bikini. She did a one-eighty, putting her back to him, gathering her hair with both hands and holding it atop her head. He tried to think of a chaste and asexual way to go about this, but it was impossible. Every fiber of his being wanted to untie her top, kiss her neck, take her hand and lead her into the bedroom. Hopefully this would be as trying as today got, so he went ahead and got to work.

The first touch on her shoulders felt innocent enough. Sure, her skin was impossibly soft and even more shimmery with the lotion on it, but he could take it. The second touch across the center of her back prompted a definite ratcheting of tension in his body. The tie of her bathing suit was right there, millimeters from his fingertips, and everything about her was so damn inviting. The third touch, however, against her lower back, all the way down to the top of her bathing suit bottoms… Well, that felt as sexual as anything Zane had done since yesterday when he'd had to pleasure himself in search of some relief.

"Don't miss a spot," she said, looking back over her shoulder.

If only she knew that was not the danger. He wasn't about to miss even a fraction of an inch. Wanting to get on with their hike and swim, and get himself out of this situation, he finished up as quickly but as thoroughly as possible. "All set."

"Thanks. Let me just grab my sun hat." She flitted off and was back a few seconds later.

They headed outside, up the beachline away from both of their cottages. At first, their walk was nothing more than a leisurely stroll along the sand, but then the coast got rocky in patches, and they would wade through knee- to waist-high water to get past the tougher terrain. A few times, they hiked inland and made their way on footpaths that wound through the forest.

"You sure you know where you're going?" Zane trailed behind Allison as they walked down a narrow trail under dense tree cover. It was a welcome break from the sun and the heat of the day. "We haven't seen a single person or even another cottage this whole time."

"Yep. I know this trip like the back of my hand. I promise. Scott and I did this a hundred times when we were kids."

"The resort has been in your family that long?"

"Yes. It originally belonged to my grandparents, but it was a little more rustic when we were growing up. The bungalows weren't quite so fancy. They didn't have all of the amenities they do now. My aunt and uncle made it into what it is today."

Ahead, Zane saw the bright sun breaking through the trees. "Is that where we're going?"

She turned back and flashed her smile at him, the one that made it hard to think straight. "Yep."

"Awesome." Zane took stock of their surroundings as soon they were out of the wooded area and back on the beach. To his right, the coast was again rocky, with a steep and densely overgrown hillside racing up from it. He then looked out over the water, spotting a tiny island. It appeared to be about the length of four or five football fields away. It had three palm trees on it but no other signs of life. "What's that?"

"That's where we're going if you're up for the swim. Scott and I named it Mako Island."

"As in the shark? Because I was more in the mood for colorful tropical fish today. Not so much into man-eating aquatic specimens."

Allison laughed. "Scott was really into sharks when we named it, but don't worry. I've never seen anything too scary in these waters."

"Oh. Okay."

"It'll take about twenty minutes to get over there, but it's an easy swim and you'll get a beautiful view the whole way. Just follow me."

Zane nodded in agreement, declining to say that if he was following her, it wasn't the ocean that would be providing the beauty. That was all on Allison.

Zane and Allison put on their fins and snorkel masks, then she grabbed the inflatable swim buoy her uncle had left for her. With a belt that went around her waist, it would float behind her, hold a few bottles of water and could double as a flotation device if either she or Zane got into trouble during their swim.

"Your aunt and uncle think of everything, don't they?" Zane asked.

"They love to be protective." Always. But she

wasn't going to let things like her family come between her and a good day with Zane. "Come on."

Allison waded into the sea, feeling so blissfully
at home the instant she was floating in the water.
They swam at a leisurely pace, buoyed by the sa-
line. Below, the ocean floor was dotted with clusters
of starfish, while schools of fish in bright shades of
yellow and blue darted between the sea plants. One
thing Allison loved more than anything about snorkeling was that the only thing she could hear was her
own breath. She purposely made it deep and even,
forcing every stress in her life from her body. Today
was for her and Zane. She'd waited fifteen years for
it to happen.

As they approached Mako Island, the water became quite shallow—only two or three feet deep.
That allowed them to walk the final fifty yards to
dry land, or in this case, what was really a very large
sandbar with a few rocks, trees and plants.

They both collapsed when they reached a shady
spot on the beach, sitting down and taking off their
fins. "That was incredible," Zane said, a bit breathless. She tried not to watch the rise and fall of his en-
ticing chest. She tried not to think about how badly
she wanted to touch him there. "Thank you so much
for sharing it with me."

"Of course. I'll give you the quick tour of the island. It won't take long." Indeed, it was only about
the size of the combined footprint of five or six Rose

Cove cottages. Mostly sand and rocks, some low brush and a half dozen palms. Unfit for human life, it wasn't completely uninhabited. Plenty of birds were busy up in the trees, and there were even a few iguanas, who could make the swim from Rose Cove or other nearby islands.

They found their way back to that shady, cool spot on the beach and took a breather. "You know, half of the fun of this is getting to show it off to someone I care about."

Zane sat forward, resting his forearms on his knees and looking down at the sand, and nodded. "That's a nice thing to say." His voice was so burdened it made her heart heavy. Why did he have to be so deeply conflicted about every nice thing she chose to say? "I care about you, too."

She had too many words on the tip of her tongue—things about her brother or other women or why in the hell he couldn't just give in to the attraction that she had to believe he felt. There was no way that the electricity between them only went one way. But she didn't want their conversation to get too serious, so she kept these nagging, negative thoughts to herself. Instead, she fished the bottles of water out of the small pouch attached to the swim buoy and handed one to Zane. "Here. Drink. I need to keep you safe out here. Scott will never forgive me if you die of dehydration."

Zane laughed. It was deep and throaty and sexy as

ever. "Same for you. I think we're equally responsible for each other at this point." He took a long drink of his water, then replaced the cap and reclined back in the sand, resting on his elbows. "It's so amazing to think about, isn't it?"

"What? How my brother has an ironclad hold on both of us?"

"Well, that, sure, but that's a long conversation. I was talking more about the here and now. When we met, did you ever think that you and I would end up together on this tiny uninhabited island in the Caribbean?"

Allison hugged her knees to her chest and ran her hands through the sand, too embarrassed to tell Zane that she'd spent more than a decade crafting fantasies about him. Of the many times she'd felt like a naive schoolgirl around him, this moment might have been the most striking. It felt as though there was an invisible force between them, keeping them apart, and she didn't know how to get rid of it. "Hard to believe, huh?"

"We're so far away from it all. From everyone. From responsibility and expectations. From family and our jobs. I had no idea it would be so freeing."

Freeing. This scenario they'd found themselves in should've felt freeing, but they didn't have true freedom, and they wouldn't unless she finally shook loose the words buzzing in her head and forced the conversation. "We could do whatever we want, you know. Nobody can say a thing."

Zane was quiet for a few heartbeats, and Allison braced for a reprimand about being suggestive. "So true. We are the extent of the society on this island." Just then, an iguana jumped up onto a rock a few dozen feet away. "Well, us and that guy."

"He won't care what we do. We could scream at the top of our lungs if we wanted to and nobody could say a thing."

"Or you could sing too loud. It might drive out the wildlife, but you could do it."

She smacked him on the arm. "Hey. I'm not that bad a singer."

"Let's just say that fifty percent of the people on this island disagree with that statement."

Allison swiped at him again, but this time, Zane ducked away before her hand could connect with his arm. He popped up onto his feet. Allison did the same. He ran into the water up to his knees and she followed in close pursuit. Before she knew what was happening, he turned and, with both hands, delivered a tidal wave of a splash, dousing her.

"Hey!" Allison protested, but she loved the playful turn Zane was taking. "That's not fair." She ran into the surf up to her waist, furiously broadcasting water back at him. He joined in and they splashed each other like crazy for a good minute, laughing and trying to outdo each other. "Okay. Okay. Truce." Allison sucked in frantic, deep breaths.

Zane relented and straightened to his full height. He was like a god standing there in the crystal clear sea, tanned and glistening with water. "I'm officially soaked." He walked several steps into the shade of a palm tree over the water, still standing in it up to his knees.

"Me, too." Allison was determined to not make the first move, even when ideas of what do with wet bathing suits were whizzing around in her head. Still, she wasn't going to avoid him. She inched closer, stepping out of the sunlight. Their gazes connected, and she reckoned with how apparent his inner conflict was. It was all over his face. It hurt to see it—he had good and valid reasons for not wanting anything physical with her. She admired those reasons. She also wished they didn't exist, or at the very least, that they could set them aside for a while.

"You're pretty when you're wet."

Something in her chest fluttered—the physical manifestation of years of wanting to hear words like the ones he'd just uttered. "Thank you. You don't look bad yourself."

He cleared his throat, and a blush crossed his face. He looked down at the water. "Your brother would kill me for what I'm thinking right now."

Her heart galloped to a full sprint. "And he's not here."

Zane returned his sights to her and tapped his finger against his temple. "Unfortunately, he's here." He then pointed to the vicinity of his heart. "And in here."

"That's so sweet. And I get it. I do." She shuffled her feet ahead on the sandy bottom.

"Do you? Really?"

"I do. You love my brother. He loves you. I admire the hell out of your friendship." She sucked in a deep breath, hoping that she could summon the courage to say what she would always regret if she didn't let it out. "But I also know that I'm incredibly attracted to you, Zane. And judging by what you just said about the thoughts going through your head, I'm reasonably sure you're attracted to me. If I'm wrong, you could save us both a lot of time by saying it. Then we can go on with the rest of our vacation as nothing more than friends."

"I'm attracted to you. A lot."

She was thankful for the forward progress, but she wanted more. She needed to seize this moment. "I'm glad. Relieved, actually."

"You had to know that."

She shrugged. "A girl likes to hear that she's pretty. That a guy is attracted to her. It's not rocket science, Zane. I'm glad you confessed what you're thinking."

"Do you want to know what I'm really thinking?"

Words seemed impossible. All she could do was nod enthusiastically.

Zane then did the thing she'd been waiting a decade for. He gave her a sign that he wanted this, too, by taking a single step closer. "You're so beautiful. I just want to see you. All of you."

Goose bumps blanketed her arms and chest, even in the warm breeze. She swallowed hard. Without a word, she reached back and pulled the string on her bikini top. As the knot fell loose, she lifted the garment over her head and tossed it up onto the sand. "Like this?"

It was his turn to move closer again, his eyes first scanning her face, then shifting to travel all over her body, looking hungry, but he would likely never know that whatever lust he was feeling for her wasn't even a fraction of what she felt for him. "Yes. Like that."

She took another step. Mere inches separated their feet. Their legs and stomachs. Her breasts were only a whisper away from his unbelievable chest. "Do you want to know what's going through *my* head?" She loved the way his lips twitched at the question.

"It would make my life so much easier if you told me."

A tiny laugh escaped her lips, but there was no mistaking the gravity of this moment. "I want you to touch me." The words came out with little effort. She'd been practicing them in her head for eons.

He raised his hand slowly, his palm facing her breast. Her nipples gathered tight in anticipation. He breached the sliver of space between them, his warm and slightly rough hand covering her breast. This was not sex, not even close, but it caused such a rush of heat in her body that she gasped.

"Like this?" he asked, gently squeezing.

"Yes." Allison's need for Zane made her breasts full and heavy. Electricity was buzzing between her legs. Now that the floodgates had been opened, she didn't merely want him anymore.

She needed him.

Five

What in the world was he doing? Zane's hands were on both of Allison's magnificent breasts, and he knew the logical next steps—kissing, trunks off, bikini bottoms gone and what he could only imagine would be the hottest sex of his life. Up against a palm tree. Rolling around in the warm sand. As amazing as that sounded, there was part of him that was terrified to go there. The temptation of forbidden fruit was no joke—he already had an erection that was not going to go away without some effort on somebody's part. He never should've started this by touching her, but the look on Allison's face right now, eyes half-closed in absolute pleasure, was such a turn-on, he wanted to get lost in it.

"Allison, I want to kiss you."

"I want you to kiss me." Her reply was swift and resolute.

He sucked in a deep breath as the ocean breezes blew his hair from his forehead. He dipped his head lower and closed his eyes, not thinking about anything other than doing what felt good. His lips met hers, and it was like tossing a match on a pile of tinder—her mouth was so soft and sexy. So giving and perfect. It was everything he could ever want from a kiss as her tongue swept along his lower lip. She popped up onto her tiptoes and leaned into him, telling him with a simple shifting of weight how badly she wanted him. But to punctuate the gesture, she reached around and grabbed his backside with both hands, pulling his hips sharply into hers. His body responded with a tightening between his legs that left him dizzy.

Allison flattened both hands on his pecs and spread her fingers wide, curling the tips into his muscles while peering up at him. "I want you, Zane. I want every inch of you."

"Here? Now?"

She slid her hands across his chest away from each other and turned her attention to points south. His swim trunks were fully tented. "I hate to make either of us wait, but I don't want to do this in the sand. The beach is beautiful, but one of our beds would be even better."

Zane didn't want to put anything on pause now that he'd made his decision. Everything between his legs was screaming at him to argue her point. But it might be wise to hold off until they could get back. It would give Allison a chance to change her mind. Zane could endure his inner tug-of-war some more. Then, if he and Allison still ended up in bed, he'd know in his heart that it hadn't been a rash decision.

She grabbed his hand. "Come on. We can get back to my cottage in a half hour if we hurry."

Disappointingly, while Zane collected their gear, Allison put her bikini top back on. They sat together in the shallow water, donning their fins. As he stood, something in the view of Rose Cove caught his eye—a sprawling white house atop the big hill rising from the beach where they'd embarked on their snorkeling trip. "Who stays up there?" he asked as they walked through the shallower depths. "I thought Hubert and Angelique lived in the main house, where the office is."

"That's the honeymoon cottage. It's undergoing renovations. They're giving it a serious face-lift. It'll probably run five grand a night when they're done."

"Wow."

"I know. I'm hoping to see the progress before we leave."

"I'd like to see it, too."

"For now, you and I need to swim." Allison pulled down her mask, adjusted the straps, plugged the snorkel end into her mouth and, like a frogman, dived into the deeper waters.

Zane followed, and this time they swam at a far less leisurely pace. Now the fish were dots of color as they zoomed past. Zane was focused on their destination until Allison came to a stop, treading water and pointing ahead. Zane scanned the depths, only to see a sea turtle come into his frame of vision. They floated in place, masks in the water as the massive creature glided toward them, then turned when it got too close, graceful, beautiful and all alone. Zane had never spent any time at all thinking about what it might be like to be a sea turtle, but he was struck by how apt the phrase "just keep swimming" was. To survive, all one could do was keep moving forward. His breaths came slow and even as he realized that he might be better served to get out of his own head every now and then and actually enjoy his life.

He and Allison watched as the turtle skated away, waiting until he was well out of sight before resuming their trek. It took very little time before they reached the beach and scooped up the rest of their belongings, including Allison's hat. She urged him ahead with a wave. "Come on. I know a shortcut through the forest."

He hustled behind her. It wasn't long before he saw her cottage through the trees. "Why didn't we go this way before? This is so much shorter."

"I wasn't in a hurry then."

When they arrived at Allison's cottage and they stepped through the door, Allison wasted no time, rising up on her tiptoes and kissing him deeply, digging her fingers into the hair at his nape. That kiss swept aside the doubts and questions he had about whether or not this was a good idea. That erection from before? It sprang to life in seconds flat as he returned the kiss and wrapped his arms around her naked waist. It felt impetuous. And dangerous. And for once in his life, he was ready to take caution and run it into the ground. Nobody had to know. This moment was all about Allison and him.

She wrenched her mouth from his, gazing up at him, her eyes wild and scanning. She probably thought he was about to bail on her like he had at Scott's birthday, but he would not do that. Not this time. He scooped her up in his arms and carried her off to the bedroom.

"How chivalrous of you," she said.

"I try," he quipped back.

He set her on her feet, and she turned her back to him, lifting her hair and letting him do what he'd wanted to do so badly before—tug on the strings of her top. With the garment gone, he reached around and cupped her breasts, which fit so perfectly in his hands. A breathless sigh left her lips, and he knew he was on the right track. He wanted to please her so much that she had no choice but to make that sound over and over again. Allison pressed her bottom against his groin, wagging her hips back and forth, cranking up the pressure already raging in his hips and belly. She craned her neck to kiss him. Their tongues teased each other, wet lips skimming and playing.

"You're so damn sexy," he whispered, moving to her glorious neck. It wasn't merely a nice thing to say. It was the truth. Every soft curve of her body had him turned on.

She hummed her approval, dropping her head to one side. He ran his lips over every available inch, exploring the delicate skin beneath her ear and the graceful slope down to her shoulder. Her unbelievable smell, sweet jasmine and citrus, mixed with the salt of sea air, filling his nose and leaving him a little drunk, although everything about Allison was intoxicating. Her voice, her words, her touch...

He shifted his hands to her hips and with a single tug at both strings, undid her bikini bottoms. She wriggled a bit and they dropped to the floor. He pressed his hand against her silky smooth belly, inching lower until he reached her center. She was slick with heat, and Allison gasped when he touched her, reaching up and back to wrap her fingers around his neck. With his other hand he caressed her breast lightly, loving the velvety texture of her skin against his palm, teasing her pert nipple, as he returned his lips to her neck. Her breaths were labored and short and, judging by the sound, she was close to her peak, but he wanted to savor this time with her. He didn't want to rush. There had been so much buildup to this moment, and he was certain it could never happen again. He wanted to appreciate this time with sweet and sinfully sexy Allison.

As if she knew what he was thinking, she turned in his arms and grabbed both sides of his head, pulling him closer in a kiss that put every other one to shame. Mouths open and hungry, wet and hurried, it was as if she was acknowledging that they could only travel this path once, and they had to make it count. She let go of her grip on him and moved to the drawstring of his trunks, making quick work and pushing them to the floor. As soon as she wrapped her hand around his length, he knew there was a good chance he wouldn't last long. He clamped his eyes shut and walked that delicate line between relishing every firm stroke she took and trying to think about anything other than how damn hot she was. Unfortunately, his best friend popped into his mind, but he quickly banished the thought. He would not disappoint her. Not today.

Again he scooped her up in his arms, but this time, he laid her out on the bed. The vision of her soft and sumptuous naked body, his for the taking, reminded him that he was a fool for wanting anything less than hours of getting lost in her. One time didn't have to mean a short time. They could make memories in this room.

She grinned as he allowed himself the luxury of her beauty. "Coming to bed?" She swished her hands across the crisp white sheets.

All he could think about was that this was the exact fantasy he'd had the other day. And now he got to live it. He was a ridiculously lucky man right now. "Just try to stop me."

Allison could hardly believe this was happening, except that it was. Her body was buzzing with appreciation for Zane and the glee of finally having a taste of what she'd wanted for so long. Judging by his opening act, she was in for an unbelievable afternoon… and, hopefully, evening. She wondered if she could convince him to never get out of bed, or if they did, to switch to the sofa in the living room. Or the kitchen counter. Or the plunge pool. *Ooh, yes.* She wanted Zane everywhere.

But she couldn't let her silly brain get so far ahead. *Go with it. Enjoy him.*

"Scoot back, darling." Zane gestured for her to move, then set his knee on the bed. Even now, when they still hadn't done the actual deed, she knew that this had been so worth the wait. All those years of pining were about to pay off. It made her heart swell, her lips tingle and her entire body reverberate.

She did as he asked and slid herself back until her head was on the pillow. Zane was now on both knees at her feet, dragging his fingers along the insides of her calves and down to the arches of her feet. Being totally naked and exposed to him like this was so exhilarating that the goose bumps came back. She liked being vulnerable with him. It made her realize exactly how much she trusted him. Not knowing what he would do next added another level of thrill. It would be so easy to chalk all of these feelings up to this being the first time, except that this was the first time with Zane, the one guy she'd always wanted.

He gripped her ankles with both hands and spread her legs wider. His eyelids were heavy, like he was drunk on appreciation for her body, and that was such a boost to her ego she could hardly wrap her head around it. She lapped up every nanosecond of the image. He leaned down and kissed the inside of her knee, then began to move his way up her thigh, in absolutely no rush, holding his lips against her skin for a heartbeat or two each time. She arched her back in anticipation of where he was going. She had not banked on him wanting to take on the oral exam, but she should've known all along that he would not only want to please her, but that he would know exactly how to do it.

She squirmed when his fingers grazed her center again and he urged her thighs apart with his forearms. She watched for a moment in awe as he used his mouth, but the pleasure became too much. She had to shut her eyes. Her head drifted back onto the pillow, and all she could do was express her appre-

ciation with moans and single-syllable words like
yes and *more*. She'd never imagined he had such an
artistic side, but the man was playing her perfectly,
with firm pressure from his lips and steady circles
from his tongue. The tension had already been building when he drove a finger inside her and curled it
against her most sensitive spot. Three or four passes
and she felt the dam break, and warm contentment
washed over her. She combed her fingers into his
hair, massaging his scalp to show her appreciation.

"That was unbelievable," she said, knowing that
the words didn't come close to telling him how she
truly felt. She would need time to process what had
just happened. For now, her brain was in frothy,
happy disarray.

He raised his head and smiled with smug satisfaction, then kissed her upper thigh. "I enjoyed it, too."

"Hopefully you'll enjoy the next part even more.
I need you, Zane. I need you inside me."

He planted both hands on the bed and raised himself above her, dipping his head down and kissing her
softly. She wrapped her legs around his hips, waiting
for the moment when he would finally drive inside.
He was hesitating, and she could sense it. She truly
admired the thoughtful side of him that felt that hesi-
tation, but she needed him to know that it was okay.
They could do this together, and it would be nothing
short of amazing.

"All these years I've known you and I had no idea

what talents you were hiding," she said. "You've been holding out on me, haven't you?"

He laughed quietly, but it felt forced. He nuzzled her cheek with his nose. She lowered her legs a bit and stroked the back of his thighs with her ankles. *Come on, Zane. Don't let me down.*

"I, uh…" His voice faltered.

"What is it?" She was careful to keep her voice warm and soothing. She did not want to witness another of his panics.

"I don't know."

"Don't know what?"

"I'm so sorry. So incredibly sorry." He turned away, avoiding eye contact. "I can't do this." Seeming defeated, he climbed off the bed and plucked his swim trunks from the floor.

Meanwhile, Allison was knee-deep in confusion. "Zane. What's wrong? I thought we were good."

"I thought we were, too. But I can't do it. I can't betray my best friend."

Naked on the bed and reeling from the pleasure Zane had just given her, the rejection still landed on Allison like the proverbial ton of bricks. Zane, the man she'd dreamed of for years, had just told her no. Logic said she should be incredibly hurt. Devastated. But right now, with this beautiful man still standing in her bedroom with an obvious erection, she was nothing but flat-out mad. It didn't have to be this way. And he knew it.

"Please don't do this," she said. "Don't leave."

"I have to. I'm sorry, but I do. I shouldn't be here in the first place."

His apology didn't do much to quiet her anger. "You're doing this. You're seriously putting on the brakes." She rolled onto her stomach, head and arms dangling off the side of the bed, and grabbed her sarong from the floor, where she'd tossed it earlier. Let him have a perfect view of her backside. Let him see what he was missing.

"I don't know why you're mad. From where I'm sitting, I just gave you a pretty mind-blowing orgasm."

"It *was* amazing. And not the point. I want you, Zane. All of you."

"I can't give you that. Not now."

A deep grumble was forming at the base of her throat. "Then when? Later tonight? Tomorrow morning? Please don't tell me we're going to leave this island without having sex." She wanted to applaud herself for truly putting it all out there.

"I've thought about it, and it's not a good idea. We've already gone too far."

She knew what that really meant. "You're going to let my brother come between us here? Nobody needs to know about this, Zane. Nobody. I don't kiss and tell. And I certainly wouldn't kiss and tell about you to him."

Zane turned away from her and stalked over to the

French doors. His heavy steps were born of frustration, which seemed like an awfully good argument for him getting back in bed with her. But apparently not. "*I* would know it had happened. That's all that matters. I can't violate that trust."

"I would like to know where in your friendship agreement it says that you can't sleep with your friend's sister, when she's a consenting adult and so are you."

He whipped around, his eyes full of an emotion she couldn't put a label on—it wasn't anger and it wasn't hurt. It was something in between. "It's a guy thing. Plus, you and I both know that this would be nothing more than a hookup. Is that really what you want?"

"Are you saying that because it's all you're capable of? Hookups? Why is that, Zane? Why do you seek out one-night stands with women, but never actually commit?"

"Now is not the time for us to discuss the rest of my personal life."

"Oh. Right. Because you're always beyond reproach." She was so angry, it felt as though her blood was boiling. She hated that this was her reaction, but it was the only thing that made sense right now.

"That's not what I was saying. You just came off a breakup, Allison. You told me yourself that it was bad. I'm not the cure for that. The cure for that is time."

Allison jumped off the bed and wrapped her sarong around herself, tying it at the shoulder. Her breakup had been a distant thought until then, and she didn't appreciate him bringing it up or, worse, using it against her. "I don't need to be cured. I need the chance to move on." She stormed past him into the living room. Out of habit, she picked up her phone from where she'd left it on a side table. She had a text from Kianna. Nothing of paramount importance, but she replied. She watched as the bar moved across the screen, then she got an error message. *Not delivered.* That was when she saw she had no bars. "Service is out."

"You said you were going to turn off your phone."

"Well, I didn't."

Zane's eyes went wide with disapproval, and Allison was struck with a horrible realization. This really was all a mistake. Zane still saw her as a kid. He'd always see her as Scott's little sister. He'd never think of her as an actual woman.

"I love how you just come out with it," he quipped.

"I'm being honest. I told you I'd turn it off because I knew that it would be the sensible thing to do on a vacation where you're supposed to truly relax, but the reality is that Kianna and I are just barely keeping our heads above water with our business and we have an important new client that could turn into a long-term retainer. I need to be able to work."

"Oh, give me a break. That guy you were talking to yesterday? That was not work. If it was, you wouldn't have sneaked off into your bedroom and closed the door. It's not like I know a single thing about your company or what you're doing."

Allison's heart was hammering in her chest. She'd thought it would seem reasonable that she'd want some privacy during a work call, but she had to admit to herself that it was solely because she was working for the one person on the planet Zane would hate forever. "It actually was business. I owe it to my recruits to exercise discretion. I'm sometimes going after very high-level people who already have important positions with big companies. I'm sorry if it's my regular practice to conduct those phone calls out of earshot of anyone. It's nothing personal." Except that it was, because the conversation was about Black Crescent. She regretted tacking on that last comment. Everything before it had been nothing less than the truth.

Zane reared his head back and held up his hands in surrender. "You don't have to get so angry, Allison. I'm sorry. If it really was work, I'm sorry I said anything, okay?"

She knew then that she'd overreacted, but it was only because she was so deeply frustrated. "Do you want to know why I'm so mad?" She felt her entire body vibrate from head to toe. Could she really come out with it? Tell him about the feelings that were tucked deep down inside her? These were things she'd never told anyone. Not her mom or Kianna. The pages of the diary she'd kept in high school were the only place where she'd ever come clean about Zane. And maybe that was part of her problem. She felt as though Zane needed to let go of his feelings about his past. Maybe she needed to set loose the things that kept haunting her, too. "I'm angry because over on Mako Island, and back there in my bedroom, I was so close to what I've wanted for fifteen years, and you decided to yank it all away."

Zane stood there, frozen, blinking like he had far more than a speck of dust in his eye. "Hold on a minute. What did you say?"

She couldn't suffer any more humiliation today. She'd had more than her fill. "You heard me. And you can feel free to go now. I just want to be left alone for the rest of my trip." She stormed off into the kitchen. That was when she saw a note on the counter. Even from across the room, she could tell it was Angelique's handwriting. She beelined for it.

Dear Allison,
I'm not sure where on the island you are, and I couldn't get a text to go through, so I'm leaving a note. Hubert was having chest pains, so I've taken him to the doctor in Nassau. Don't worry. This has happened before. I think it's stress. I considered staying on Rose Cove, but I wanted to be with him, and our remaining guests have

*opted to leave because of the weather. I don't
think the storm will hit the island, but we will
feel some of its effects. I would not leave if I
didn't think it was safe for you and Zane to be
here. You have lived through many storms at
Rose Cove and know what to do. Stay safe and
hunker down if necessary. I'm sure Hubert and
I will be back on the island tomorrow.
Love, Angelique*

Zane hadn't left her cottage as Allison had asked.
In fact, he was standing right behind her. "Have you
looked outside? The sky is getting menacing. I guess
we didn't notice it since we walked back inland in
the shade."

"The weather can turn on a dime here." Allison
handed him the note from her aunt. "And we were
busy for a little while after that, too." She watched
as Zane scanned the note.

"Whoa. I hope your uncle is okay."

"Yeah. Me, too." Everything about this day had
gone so wrong. Right now, she just wanted to go
to bed and try to sleep it off. "Not much we can do
right now but wait."

"But the storm. Don't you think we should figure
out what's going on?"

She'd been through dozens of false alarms with
storms on this island. The weather was the least of

her worries. "You do whatever you want, Zane. For me, I'm going to get some sleep and try to forget that you don't want to have sex with me."

Six

By late the next morning, the rain was coming down in torrential sheets, and Zane was deeply concerned about what might be in store for Allison and him on Rose Cove. He couldn't get a signal on his phone. The other resort guests were all gone. Zane had been to the dock several times, hoping there would be a boat there, but he'd had no luck. Either they'd missed them all or no one was coming to get them. Angelique had told Allison to hunker down, but Zane wanted to make one more attempt to look for a way off this island. And he wasn't going without Allison. He had to keep her safe. Even if she hated him, he was going to drag her along.

He trudged down the beach to her cottage, rain pelting his entire body while the wind pushed against him, forcing Zane to dig his feet deeper into the sand with each step. His thighs burned from the effort; his skin stung from the sheets of rain. He squinted through the drops but could see up on Allison's patio. Her doors and windows were closed. Once he arrived at her back door, Allison was nowhere in sight, so he had to knock. As he waited for an answer, he turned back to the ocean. The waves that had been so lovely and calm a day or two ago were now starting to rage. The water was at a full-on churn like a washing machine. Best-case scenario as far as Zane could guess would be that the storm would only skirt the Bahamas and they wouldn't sustain a direct hit. But with no access to a forecast, it was impossible to know what they were waiting for, whether this was as bad as things would get or if this was only the beginning.

He turned back to the door and pounded again. "Come on, Allison. Answer the damn door." Impatient, he turned the knob and stepped inside just as she stumbled out of her bedroom.

"Zane. What the hell? You just walk in here? I was taking a nap. There's nothing else to do with this weather."

Zane hated how beautiful she looked. He especially hated the way his entire body had gone warm and his face had flushed. He might have been struck by a sudden case of best-friend guilt yesterday, but that didn't change the fact that he wanted her badly. "It's getting worse out there, and I have no cell service, so I don't know what's going on. Are you able to get any bars?"

"Oh, this from the guy who criticized me for using my phone." She turned on her heel and retreated to her bedroom.

He had no choice but to follow her. "Don't be mad about yesterday. This is important."

She was standing in front of her dresser, staring at her phone. The bed was disheveled, and good God he wanted to scoop her up and lay her down on it. But this was no time for that. "I'm planning on being mad about yesterday for as long as I feel like it." She held her phone up over her head at a different angle, then off to the side. "And no. I'm not getting any bars, either."

Zane still wasn't sure he'd heard her correctly yesterday afternoon when she'd said that thing about him taking away the thing she'd wanted for fifteen years. Was it really possible that she'd had some sort of crush on him all that time? And if so, what in the world was he supposed to do about that?

"I think we should grab our stuff and camp out by the marina in the hopes that somebody shows up."

She cast a look at him that said she thought he was an idiot. "There's no shelter out by the dock. We'd literally be standing there in the rain. Quite possibly forever."

"Do you have a better idea? I have to think that your aunt and uncle are worried about you. That they would try to send someone to get you."

"Angelique and Hubert have a lot on their plates right now, and they know the weather here better than anyone." She closed her eyes tightly and shook her head. "Now, the rest of my family is another case. I don't even want to think about Scott right now. He's probably losing it."

There was that name again—the reason for this state of torture he was in with Allison. "They're probably all worried sick. I'm also thinking there's no way they'll let you stay here if there's a way to safely get you back. Which is why I think we need to stay as close to the dock as possible."

"Okay. Fine. Let's go. It'll just take me a minute to pack up."

"Perfect. I'll be back in five." Zane ran over to his place as fast as the rain and wind would allow, and chucked everything into his backpack. By the time he returned, Allison was waiting for him.

"This is a terrible end to what should have been a perfect vacation," she said.

Somehow, Zane sensed that she wasn't merely talking about the weather. "I know. But I'm not going to die out here, and I'm not going to let anything happen to you, either." Not thinking, he took her hand and led them around to the path that would eventually take them to the main office. When they arrived up at the clearing, the ground was littered with palm fronds. The trees were bowing with every new gale. "The wind is only going to get worse," he called out, still pulling her along.

"I'm not worried about wind so much as I'm worried about the water. If there's a big storm surge, the sea level will rise considerably. Ten feet. Maybe more. I don't know how smart it is to wait by the dock."

She had a point. When Falling Brook was hit by Hurricane Sandy, the storm surge had been overwhelming, flooding countless homes and businesses. People had died. It had been a disaster in every sense of the word. "We have to find a way to leave a message at the dock to let someone know we're still here, but then we need to find the high point of the island."

"That's going to be the honeymoon cottage up on the hill. The one they're renovating."

"Won't we be sitting ducks up there? If there are tornadoes, it could pluck the building off the top of the cliff and toss it out into the sea." It seemed that no matter what they did, they were in deep trouble.

"It's somewhat protected, because the back side of the building is built into the rocks. And it's on the western side of the island, where the winds won't be quite as strong."

"You really know a lot about hurricanes."

"My brother is a weather nerd."

"Okay, well, let's focus on the message first.

Any ideas?" Zane asked, setting his backpack on the ground for a moment.

Allison let go of her small overnight bag and started untying her sarong. She was wearing the same bikini top, but this time with shorts.

"I'm not sure what kind of message you're trying to send," he blurted. This was not the time for him to have another moral crisis prompted by Allison disrobing.

"Everyone who works on this island has seen me wearing this. I'll tear it into strips and we'll tie those onto trees to lead someone up to the honeymoon cottage. We'll start with one of the metal pilings on the dock. Hopefully that will be enough of a signal that we're still here."

"Do you really want to rip that up? You love it."

Allison pulled at the fabric until it gave way and she was able to get a strip of it free. "I don't love this thing more than I love being alive." She waved him ahead as she made off in the direction of the small marina. "Come on."

Zane's mind raced as he struggled to keep up and surveyed the island landscape—the wild rustle of the palms above them and the constant sideways pelting of the rain making it seem like they were on another planet right now. It certainly felt like a different place than it had been twenty-four hours ago. This was paradise upended. Gone was the calm serenity he had sought.

They jogged ahead, breaking out from under the canopy of shade only to learn how much the trees had been blocking the wind. Allison's hair whipped like crazy. Ahead, the ocean's churn was an endless sloshing of unfathomable amounts of water. Gone was the crystalline blue. This sea was coal gray and angry. The whitecaps and foam were of no consolation; they only served as a reminder that things were not as they should be. And against that tumultuous backdrop was Allison, looking tiny and defenseless running toward the dock, even when Zane knew very well that she was as tough as nails. If anyone was well suited to survive, it was her. Zane felt as though he was still honing the skill, but he would be damned if this storm was going to hurt her. Not on his watch. Not while he had anything to say about it.

He hustled to catch up. They arrived at the dock, which was now nothing more than a series of gray wood planks nearly submerged in the water. There was no boat, nor were there any other people. Zane now doubted that anyone would be coming for them despite Allison's family's concern for her safety. The seas were too rough. It was all too dangerous.

Allison carefully started down the dock and Zane followed right behind her, just in case she slipped. They both pitched to the side with every wave that threatened to swallow up the slick wood planks beneath their feet. Zane again told himself that he would not let anything happen to her. He had to keep Allison safe. Still, he knew that fighting Mother Nature was a losing proposition. If she decided she was going to win, there was not much to be done.

About halfway down the dock, the water was getting even deeper and Allison smartly came to a stop. She took the strip of sarong and wrapped it around the metal pole that moored the structure to the seafloor. On a calm day, this would have been a simple task, but it was pure chaos outside right now. With her hands occupied and the wind threatening to topple her, even while she used her strong legs to brace herself, Zane had no choice but to wrap one arm around her waist, steadying her while pressing his body into hers. She felt too good against him. Too right. And maybe it was the adrenaline coursing through his veins that made him think that if ever there was a time to throw caution to the wind, it was now, when life was hanging in the balance and they had no idea if they were going to survive.

Allison couldn't take any more of Zane's hands around her waist. It was too great a reminder of everything she couldn't have. She pried herself away from him now that the fabric was tied to the dock piling. She ran along the planks, but lost her footing at the very end. With a definitive *thud*, she landed on her butt. Pain crackled through her hip and down her thigh.

"Dammit!" She scrambled to her knees, embarrassed, frustrated and several other unpleasant emotions. She attempted to stand, but the dock was like a skating rink, and the ocean wasn't playing nice, either, sloshing water in her face.

"Let me help you." Zane threaded his hands under her armpits and lifted her to her feet with what seemed like zero effort.

"I can take care of myself." She twisted her torso and leaped up onto the sand.

"I'm well aware of that. It doesn't mean I can't still help you. If anything ever happened to you, Scott would never forgive me."

Allison was so tired of this. She turned to Zane, planting a single finger in the center of his chest to put him on notice. "I don't want to hear one more word about what my brother will or will not forgive you for. If I die in this storm—which, for the record, I know I will not—I will take all of the blame. You are officially recused of your bro duties."

He grabbed her hand with both of his. "But you'll be dead, so I will definitely get blamed."

"Then my ghost will haunt you and Scott and make sure you both know it was all me. Now, come on, let's finish leaving our trail of fabric." Allison didn't wait for him to respond and trekked up to the spot where they'd dropped their bags next to the trail that led to the clearing. She tore off another piece of the sarong and handed it to Zane, pointing to a tree branch she couldn't reach.

He tied it off. "We should go get whatever food we can and bring it up the hill with us."

She didn't want to give him any credit at all right now, but that was an excellent call. She hadn't thought twice about food since yesterday, too miserable over his rejection. "Good idea."

"Thanks." He smiled, which seemed like more of an apology than anything.

Allison wasn't quite ready to accept that from Zane, spoken or otherwise. So she started walking.

They split up back at their cottages, each scavenging for supplies. Allison took a moment to use a pair of scissors she found in her kitchen to cut up the rest of her sarong, but she still managed to return to their meetup spot first with bananas, bread, a flashlight and a blanket.

Zane emerged from his place second. "I brought a bottle of champagne."

Allison just shook her head. "I'd say you were a numbskull if I didn't need a drink so badly right now."

"For what it's worth, I also brought cheese and crackers, apples and a deck of cards."

"Great. It'll be just like summer camp." Chances were that it might be just as rustic up the hill. She had no idea what they were walking into, whether the solar was connected up there and whether they'd have furniture to sit or sleep on.

They retraced the inland path they had taken yesterday, stopping periodically to tie another piece of her sarong to a tree. Having some protection from the rain and wind made the trip much easier than it would have been near the raging ocean, but it was still slow going. The ground seemed to shake with every gust of wind, rain was still coming down in sheets and they were both completely soaked. Allison didn't necessarily fear for her life, but she was scared of the unknown right now. She was reasonably certain that she and Zane could work together as a team to survive, but what toll would it take on her heart when this was all over? A huge one, she feared. She was going to need a vacation from her vacation.

When they reached the base of the hill, it looked like an almost insurmountable climb. She was already exhausted and dreading what it was going to be like, holed up inside a shell of a house while riding out the storm. Even worse, the spot on her hip where she'd fallen was throbbing. "I'm really not excited about doing this," she said.

"Seriously? You? The woman who marched me all over this island and had me snorkeling long distances?"

"Seriously. Me." Deep down, the real reason she wasn't looking forward to getting herself up the hill had nothing to do with exhaustion. Yesterday, she could stay away from Zane in her own space. How was she supposed to do that when they were about to be living in tight quarters and having to rely on each other to survive?

"It's okay. We can do it. We just need to get to shelter." He peered down at her, and all she could think was that this was such a damn shame. He was perfect. The two of them together for a night or two could have been magical. But no.

"Yeah. Okay. Let's do this." She led him down a narrow path at the foot of the hill, which eventually brought them to a wider trail that zigzagged its way up the incline. The terrain was mostly low scrub, giving them zero protection from the wind and rain. They both walked with heads down, watching the trail, slogging through what was quickly becoming a muddy mess.

"Is it just me or is the weather getting worse?" Zane asked as they made the final turn on the trail. They were close.

"It is. I wish we had access to an actual forecast. It would be nice to know if this was going to be the worst of it or if it's only the beginning. I hope this hike won't end up being for nothing."

"Better safe than sorry, right?"

She shrugged. "You can't spend your whole life staying out of trouble."

"Why do I have the feeling we aren't talking about the storm anymore?"

She came to a stop at the end of the trail, turned and confronted him. Water was running down her nose and cheeks. She felt like a drowned rat. "We aren't."

Zane's shoulders dropped in defeat. "Allison, come on. I don't want to argue."

"I don't, either, Zane. I shouldn't have to." Allison trudged her way around to the front of the house via a crushed-shell path with manicured hedges on either side. Bright pink bougainvillea was trailing from planters situated between the windows of the house. It had been years since she'd been up here, and she had no idea what state the house would be in, but the exterior already looked much nicer than she'd ever remembered, even in the pouring rain.

When they rounded to the front of the house, they both froze, even though they were standing in a complete downpour.

"Holy crap, Allison."

She didn't have a great response. It was beyond words. "I know." There was so much to take in, it was difficult to figure out where to start. First, either she hadn't appreciated the view when she was younger or it had somehow gotten better over the years. From this vantage point, you could see for miles, even with the disastrous weather. The glassy azure ocean was gone, replaced by a tumultuous cobalt sea, but it was still a sight to behold, and somehow seemed less menacing all the way up here.

And then there was the house. From the outside,

everything was definitely upgraded from the last time she'd been up here. The old tiny plunge pool had been replaced with a sprawling one, complete with an infinity edge and surrounded by a gorgeous patio. If she wasn't already as wet as she could possibly be, Allison would've jumped right in.

They ducked under the sizable porch roof. "I'm confused," Zane said. "I thought you said they were renovating. I don't know what the exterior used to look like, but it seems pretty damn perfect to me. The pool's full of water."

"They *were* renovating. Or at least that's what I thought, although I didn't actually speak to Angelique about it before I came down. It wasn't like I was going to be staying in the honeymoon villa." Nor would she be staying here again anytime soon. Her romantic future looked as bleak as could be, hot on the heels of rejection by not one, but two men. First Neil and his cheating ways, and then she attempted to distract herself with Zane, which didn't work at all. Maybe she needed to just give up on men entirely. Focus on her career. The financial and professional upside with Black Crescent was potentially huge, and now that she wasn't quite as concerned with hurting Zane's feelings, she could really put her foot on the gas when they finally got out of this mess of a storm.

Zane turned and cupped his hands at his temples, peering into one of the windows. "Uh. Allison. It looks pretty spectacular inside, too."

She strode over to one of the French doors and turned the knob, then stepped inside. "Wow. Gorgeous."

The space was light and airy, twice the size of either of their cottages, but with one noticeable difference—the bed was right in the main living space. Situated on a platform that spanned the long back wall of the building, it had a soaring canopy overhead and sumptuous white linens. Allison walked across the room and took the two steps up onto the raised area, still several feet from the bed.

Zane was right by her side. "I guess if you're on your honeymoon, there's no reason to think about being anywhere other than in the sack."

"Yeah. I guess." She had to wonder what that would be like, to be so enamored of someone that you wouldn't even bother to get out of bed. The only person she'd ever imagined that with was Zane, and she already knew that wasn't going to happen.

"That bed looks so damn good," she muttered. "I just want to take a nap."

"You can do whatever you want, you know."

"My clothes are still wet."

"We should both change. You can have the bathroom, of course."

Of course. Allison snatched up her bag and poked her head into a doorway she assumed was the bathroom. Out of habit, she flipped the light switch. To her great surprise, the fixture over the vanity came on. "The light works," she shouted out to Zane.

"Thank God for solar," Zane called back.

This room would be gorgeous eventually, but was definitely still under construction, with the tile of the two-person walk-in shower not yet complete. It had the other creature comforts, though—running water at the sink and toilet. Allison was happy for the little things.

As soon as she pushed down her shorts, the pain in her hip flared. She took a look in the mirror. Her upper thigh was turning a deep shade of purple. "No wonder it was hurting." The thought of putting on more clothes that might bind against her injury was too unpleasant, so she put on a black sundress and skipped panties.

"Better?" Zane asked, wearing a dry pair of gray shorts and no shirt. He was currently toweling his hair and making it look like a seduction move. He was clearly oblivious to his effect on her.

She decided to save them both the lecture about how he should really be wearing more clothes. "My hip is all messed up." She lifted the hem of her dress to show the edge of her deepening bruise.

"We need to get some ice on that, stat." He made off for the kitchen.

"I doubt the fridge is working," she said, gingerly sitting at the foot of the mattress.

"Got it," Zane said, rattling a white plastic bin presumably filled with ice.

"Wow. A second round of applause for the solar."

Zane dug around in a drawer, eventually finding a towel and placing a handful of ice in it. He brought it to her. "Scoot back on the bed."

She raised both eyebrows at him. This was way too much like yesterday's invitation, and she already knew this wasn't going to end well, either. "Maybe I should sit on the floor."

"Don't be ridiculous. You're hurt. You should be resting. Scoot back and lie on your side."

She didn't have the strength to argue. Zane sat next to her on the mattress, placing the ice pack on her hip. She winced at the pain.

"Just relax," he said, grabbing a pillow for her.

She took a deep breath, extended her arm and rested her head. "Thanks."

"Looks like the rain and wind aren't letting up anytime soon."

Indeed, there were sheets of sideways drops again. They pelted the surface of the pool, creating ripples and waves. It was oddly soothing, which was nice because not much else could make her happy right now. It felt as though life was playing a cruel trick on her, sticking her in the honeymoon cottage with Zane.

"So, I wanted to ask you something," he said.

"Go for it. It's not like I have anything better to do."

"Were you serious when you said you'd been waiting fifteen years to have sex with me?"

Seven

Zane didn't enjoy putting anyone on the spot, but he'd been wondering about this since the minute Allison said it. Between that and the storm, his mind had been occupied with nothing else. Had she really had a thing for him all these years and he'd somehow managed to be oblivious? When she'd kissed him at Scott's birthday he'd assumed it was nothing more than the impetuous move of a woman who'd had a few glasses of wine with dinner. Now he was eager to find out if he'd been wrong.

Allison stared at him, shaking her head. Her talent for making him feel like an idiot was unparalleled, but she somehow managed to make it charming.

"You know, I've been thinking about it, and there's no way you're this clueless. You had to know I had a crush on you back in school. So if this is just some exercise to stroke your ego, I'm going to skip it." She snatched the ice pack from his hand, climbed off the bed and tossed the cold bundle into the freezer.

"I swear I had no idea." Of course, all those years ago, his brain had been occupied elsewhere. Women seemed to be the only thing that distracted him from the misery of his family's abrupt and complete falling apart. Plus, Allison had been totally off-limits. Scott's friendship and support had saved Zane. There was no breaking that trust, but it had been especially true at that time. "But I was pretty stuck in my own head when we were younger."

"I think you're still stuck in it." She walked back to the bedside and planted her hands on her hips.

Zane was sitting on the edge of the mattress, looking up at her, mystified. "Excuse me?"

"Your loyalty to Scott all stems from this time in your life that you aren't willing to let go of, Zane. It's not healthy. Being a good friend is one thing, but it's not like you're forever indebted to my family because we were kind to you. Because we welcomed you when things were rough. That's just what people do."

"You didn't go through what I did, Allison. You have no idea what it felt like."

She closed her eyes and pinched the bridge of her nose, as if she couldn't possibly be more frustrated with him. She chose to sit next to him on the bed, which was of some consolation. "You know what? I don't know, exactly. But I do know what it's like to struggle or to get knocked down or to have a hard time. You don't have a lock on that. You need to find a way to let go of what happened. Or at least move past it."

"That's why I came to this island. To clear my head. To try to let go of my animosity toward Black Crescent and the Lowell family. Or at least some of it. I don't know that I can ever let all of it go."

"Why not? Why can't you just forgive everyone at Black Crescent for what Vernon Lowell did? It's not their fault." Allison's eyes were wild and pleading. Meanwhile, the storm outside was starting to rage like never before. The windows rattled, and rain made a thunderous chorus on the roof.

"The Lowells destroy everything. Families most of all. They ruined my family. My parents got divorced because of the things they did. And for what? So somebody who was already making way too much money as far as I'm concerned could make *more* money? I just can't forgive them for that. It's the worst kind of greed." As if Mother Nature was on his side, a massive gust of wind whipped up, smacking a massive palm frond against the French doors. He and Allison both jumped.

"Whoa," Allison said, holding a hand to her chest, breathing hard.

"It's getting scary out there." The sky blackened. It was as if the sun had been extinguished.

"I'm tired of this, Zane. So tired."

"The weather?"

She inched closer to him on the bed. "No. This. Us. We could die up here. This is serious. And I have waited for you for years."

He was still having a hard time understanding this. Years? He really had been oblivious to her feelings, and that made him feel worse. "But I didn't know. I swear."

She pressed her finger against his lips. "No. I know that now. And it makes me feel like a loser, but I don't care. I don't want to die not knowing what it's like to make love to the one guy I have always wanted."

Zane felt as though his heart was going to beat its way out of his chest. In some ways, it still felt impossible that she was talking about him. There hadn't been enough time to riffle through the memories they shared to look for hints of this crush she'd supposedly had on him. "Don't say that. Don't hold me up on a pedestal and put yourself down at the same time. You're beautiful. You're smart and amazing. You could have any guy you want."

"Any guy?"

He didn't understand the question. Had she not looked in the mirror? Did she not realize that she was not only beautiful on the outside, but on the inside, as well? "Yes. No question."

She shook her head, not taking her sights from his face. "If you think that's really true, I want you to prove it, Zane. Show me that I can have *you*."

Damn, she was clever. "I see what you did there."

"Look, I know what you're like. You don't like to feel tied down or obligated. I know you're not a forever kind of guy, but will you be mine for right now? Nobody ever has to know. Not my brother. Not anyone. I just don't want to live with this regret. I know I'm not going to get another chance."

His breaths felt as though they were being dragged from his body as Allison's warm eyes pleaded for an answer. How could he ever be good enough for her? She was everything any guy with half a brain would want. Gorgeous. Exceptionally smart. Sweet, while still standing for what she wanted. She was quite possibly the most complex and unpredictable woman he'd ever met. He cared about her. And she cared about him. These were not the circumstances under which he normally pursued sex. It was so much easier when there was nothing but physical pleasure on the line. There was more at stake here. So much more. But how could he say no to her again?

He pressed the palm of his hand against her cheek. The house shook with another gale. He watched as her eyes drifted shut and she leaned into his touch. The world was threatening to rip the rug out from under them, and she didn't care. He could see it on her stunning face as she drew in a deep breath through her nose. Warmth radiated to his hand from her silky soft cheek, and he knew then that he could not let her down. He would give in to every carnal inclination he had when it came to Allison. And he would do it because she wanted him just as badly as he wanted her.

He cupped her face with his other hand and pressed his lips against hers. They stumbled into the kiss like it was the only way forward for either of them. Her tongue swept along his lower lip, sending need right through him, like a shot to the heart. His pulse picked up, and she dug her fingers into his hair, craving, needing, curling her nails into his scalp and raking his skin. He pulled her against him and lay back on the bed, tugging her along with him. She straddled his hips and ground against his crotch with her center.

Everything in his groin went tight. His mind went blank. Need slipped into the driver's seat when she countered his weight by lifting her hips and bucking against him. He felt her smile against his lips before she got serious again, kissing him deeply and squeezing his rib cage with her knees. Zane's hands went to the hem of her dress, slipping underneath it and skimming the sides of her thighs. He sucked in a sharp breath when he realized she wasn't wearing any panties. All that time he'd spent holding the ice to her hip…he'd been so close to touching her and hadn't realized it. No wonder she'd finally put him on notice. She'd had enough.

He gripped one of her hips, but touched the other one lightly. "Does it hurt?"

She shook her head, then began to kiss his neck. "No. I don't really care about pain right now anyway. Hurt me if you need to, Zane. It's okay."

"I really don't want to."

She pressed another kiss to his lips. "I know. And I love you for it. But it's okay. I won't break."

"Promise?"

"I do." She trailed her mouth to his ear, then down his jaw and his neck, leaving a blazing white trail of heat behind as each kiss evaporated on his skin. Down the center of his chest she continued to drive him wild, her hands spreading across his pecs. Squeezing. Caressing. Exploring. He'd never had a woman show so much appreciation for every inch of him.

One leg at a time, she shifted herself between his knees. She sat back and ran one hand over the front of his shorts. That one brush of her fingers nearly drove him insane. His legs felt like they were made of rubber while his entire crotch strained with urgency. His balls drew tight. With a single finger, still through the fabric of his clothes, she drew a line from the base of his length all the way to a tip. He managed to pry open his eyes halfway for an instant—he loved the look on her face. The one that said she had him at her mercy and she was going to enjoy the hell out of this.

And he expected nothing less.

Allison didn't bother with thoughts of what might happen tomorrow or the next day. It wasn't hyperbole to say they might not ever come. The storm would take what it wanted, and so would she. So she kept her senses, her thoughts and her heart in the present—this precious moment with Zane, the one she'd waited on for so long.

She unbuttoned his shorts and shimmied them, along with his boxers, down his hips. She wrapped her fingers around his length, in awe of the tension his skin could hold. He moaned his approval as she stroked him firmly, but she knew she could do better. So much better. She could make him immensely happy.

She lowered her head and took him into her mouth, leaving her lips a little slack and letting the gentle glide of her tongue deliver the pleasure she was so eager for him to have. A deep groan left his throat, just as another mighty gust of wind made the rafters quake above them. If this was how she died, she could be happy with that. She would have had everything she'd ever wanted.

Sealing her lips around him, she built some suction, appreciating the tightness it created in his body. It radiated off him in waves. He dug his fingers into her mess of hair, but he was more encouraging with his touch than anything. He wanted her to keep going, and she did, not thinking about time, the passes of her lips slow and methodical. As his skin grew more taut, she knew that he was close to his peak. There was a temptation to drive him over the cliff, but this degree of intimacy wasn't what she'd waited for. And she wasn't about to let him get there without her.

She gently released him from her lips and sat back on her haunches. She crossed her arms in front of her and lifted the sundress over her head. The soft fabric brushed against the skin of her belly and breasts. Her nipples went tight and hard from the rush of air. She flung the garment aside, not wanting to put it back on ever.

The slyest grin crossed Zane's face as his eyes scanned her naked body. She loved feeling like his reward. It was all she'd wanted to be for so long. "Get over here."

She climbed back on top of him, straddling his hips and resting her hands on his abs. His hard erection was right between her legs, and she rocked her body forward and back, letting his tip ride over her apex. Meanwhile, she dropped her head and kissed him. She loved this all-new level of getting to know him, of being able to correctly guess when he might nip at her lower lip or tangle his tongue with hers.

Even more, she loved it when he surprised her with a squeeze or lick.

Or at the moment, by rolling her to her back. He pushed her hair away from her face and kissed her deeply, full of passion she'd never seen from him. It was as if he was putting all of the intensity of his personality into a kiss. She soaked up every minute of it while trying to match it, wrapping her legs around his waist and muscling him closer. Every inch of her body felt like it was on fire right now, burning with urgency. "I need you, Zane. I want you inside me."

"Let me get a condom." He hopped off the bed and traipsed across the room to pick up his backpack.

Allison propped herself up on her elbows, in part to watch his beautiful naked form in motion, and in part to take a peek outside. The sky was so dark it looked like midnight, but it was still afternoon. Wind rasped against the windows. The wood structure of the house creaked. But fear was nowhere in sight. She had Zane, and that was all that mattered.

He returned to the bed, tearing open the packet and rolling the condom onto his erection. He positioned himself between her legs, and she raised her hips, waiting for him. He was taking things slow. Too slow. How she disliked being treated as though she were fragile. She closed her eyes, reminding herself to stay in the moment. It was then that he came inside. Inch by inch, she felt herself mold around him. She had to look at him to keep herself locked on what was really happening, and she was gladly greeted by his incredibly handsome face.

She ran her hand over his cheek and strong jaw, loving the feel of stubble against her palm as they moved together. "You feel so good. So much better than I ever imagined."

"You actually imagined this before?"

She might die of embarrassment, but she also didn't want to lie about it. "Yes. Many times."

He grinned and kissed her softly. "Were we doing it like this?"

"Sometimes."

He lowered his head and nestled his face in the crook of her neck, resting his body weight against her center, applying the right pressure. "Tell me, Alli. Tell me more."

The tension in her body was building so fast, she was a little appalled that he expected her to answer, let alone weave together the many stories she kept in her head. "In my imagination, you're perfect. You know exactly how I like it. How deep." She bit down on her lip as he punctuated her own statement with a forceful thrust. "You know that I love feeling your mouth all over my body. My neck. My breasts."

He raised his head, kissing his way from her collarbone to her nipple, swirling his tongue around the tight and sensitive bud. "Like this?"

He switched to the other side, giving it a gentle

tug with his teeth and sending a verifiable wave of electricity right between her legs.

"Yes." *Yes yes yes yes yes.* Her breaths became sharp and short. The peak was chasing her down the way a lion seeks its prey. It wasn't just physical right now. Knowing she could say something, and that Zane would follow her cues, was almost too much. She was drunk on power and craving the release.

He took her nipple between his lips and sucked harder while taking more deep strokes. That was enough to push her over the edge, and her head thrashed back on the pillow, the delicious reward spreading through her body, wave after wave. Zane drove deeper and more deliberately, and she was still knee-deep in the pleasure when he came, burying his face in her neck and arching his back. His entire body froze for a moment before he collapsed on top of her and rolled to her side.

"That was amazing," she said, her chest still heaving. She was pretty proud of herself for putting together so many words. Her brain could hardly function right now.

"It was unbelievable. Just knowing that you thought those things about me. I had no idea it would be such a turn-on."

She immediately rolled to her side, planting her hand in the dead center of his chest. "Don't you dare make fun of me for it."

"Are you kidding? I would never do that. What

guy doesn't want a sexy woman to tell him the things she's fantasized about, especially when she's imagined doing those things with him?"

She was filled with a surprising amount of pride. "Okay. Good. I was a little worried."

His adorable smile crossed his face. He reached out and tucked a tendril of her hair behind her ear. "Don't worry. I'm just in awe of you, I swear."

She knew she was grinning like a fool. She could see the tops of her own cheeks. Her face hurt. In fact, she was so giddy, she couldn't think of a thing to say.

"What are you thinking?" He smoothed his hand over her bare belly. Even in the warm afterglow, she wanted more of him.

"That I hope we don't get rescued anytime soon. Or ever." It was the truth. She could stay here forever and be happy. She didn't need another thing in the world right now. It was a scary admission to make to herself. She knew what it meant—she'd been fooling herself when she'd decided that one time with Zane would be enough.

He smiled and laid another devastating kiss on her. "I don't want to get rescued, either."

Eight

Zane woke to the sound of her name.

"Allison!"

It had to be part of a dream, he guessed, but then she curled into him, snuggling her face against his chest, and he didn't question it. He stroked her hair and pulled her closer, inhaling her sweetness. He wanted to bottle up her smell and carry it with him everywhere.

"How do you do that?" she asked.

"Do what?" He was still drifting in and out of sleep.

"Make it sound like you're shouting at me from far away when you're actually right here."

"Huh?"

"Allison Randall! If you can hear me, say something!"

That was when Zane realized it was a man's voice calling Allison's name, and it was coming from outside the house.

Allison shook his arm. "I think someone has come to rescue us."

Still half-asleep and bleary-eyed, Zane could see that the sun was peeking between the clouds. The storm had passed. They were alive. "What? Where?" Zane sat up and shook his head to rid himself of the mental cobwebs. "Hurry. They're probably wondering where in the hell we are."

Both naked, they scrambled for their clothes. As much as Zane had hoped for a sexy morning with Allison, it appeared that was not going to happen. They raced to get dressed, Zane finishing first. He stumbled for the patio door and flung it open, rushing outside. Allison was right behind him. They rounded the house on the crushed-shell path. Several hundred yards away, Marcus, the man who had piloted the boat he took onto the island, was on his way up the hill.

Allison waved. "Marcus! Up here! We're here!"

Marcus's vision fell on her. His shoulders dropped in relief. "Your family has been worried sick!" he shouted back through cupped hands before resuming his climb.

Zane could only imagine. He'd witnessed the way

Allison's family fretted over her. Scott was probably beside himself. "I'm sorry you had to come all the way up here," Zane said when Marcus reached them. "We decided the highest point was the safest. We were worried about the storm surge and the water more than I was worried about the wind."

"Smart. You probably saved yourselves. The cottages you two were staying in both had significant flooding."

Allison's sights darted to Zane, and it was as if he could see her heart plummeting to her stomach. Her aunt and uncle would be devastated to learn of the fate of their resort, especially on the heels of her uncle's health issues. "Do you know how my uncle Hubert is doing?" she asked.

"He had a heart bypass, but he's doing well. They ended up transporting him to a hospital in Atlanta. It was too dangerous with the storm to try the surgery in Nassau or even in Miami. They didn't want to risk the power going out. But he's recovering well. Your aunt, on the other hand, has been so worried. She said she would never forgive herself if you got hurt while staying on the island. She wanted to send me back for you earlier, but the waters were too rough."

"I was very lucky to have Zane with me. He knew exactly what to do."

Zane emphatically shook his head. He wasn't about to take credit for their safety. In truth, he'd been hoping that they wouldn't be found. He and Allison had such an amazing night. Unforgettable. Most likely a once-in-a-lifetime event, which struck him with a sense of melancholy he hadn't thought to prepare himself for. "It was a joint effort. Allison came up with the idea to leave the scraps of her sarong to send a message about where we were."

"It was smart. That's exactly how I found you." Marcus tugged the final strip of sarong fabric off a nearby shrub. "Come on. Let's get your things and get you to Eleuthera and on the plane to Miami. Your brother is waiting there."

Oh, crap. This was not a good development. Zane wasn't even close to being ready to see his best friend. If Scott was worried enough to fly to Miami, he would be that much more likely to pick up on any romantic vibes between Allison and Zane. For that reason, Zane was going to have to shut it all down way before they went near Scott. The thought pained him, but it was for the best.

"Scott flew down to Miami? Was that really necessary?" Allison asked.

"Like I said. Your whole family has been extremely worried about you," Marcus said.

Zane patted Allison's arm as platonically as possible. They needed to get back to being friends *without* benefits. "It'll be okay. We're safe. That's all that matters."

Allison, Zane and Marcus forged their way back to the honeymoon villa and collected what few belongings they still had. Zane was the first inside and found himself rushing inside to make up the bed, which was pretty much a disaster. The things he and Allison had done to each other there felt like a dream. They'd been amazing in the moment, but Zane needed to get his head out of the clouds and hop back on the straight and narrow. He desperately hoped that Marcus did not have a relationship with Scott. Loose lips could sink ships, or in this case, a deeply important friendship.

It took about an hour to make it back down the hillside and across the island to the dock. There, flapping in the bright early-morning sun, was the first piece of Allison's sarong, still tied to the metal piling. She'd been collecting the strips of fabric along the way. Zane got to it first and rescued it for her.

"Maybe you can have it sewn back together," Zane said, thinking that if he could have anything right now, it would be one more chance to see her wearing it. But he needed to stop thinking of Allison that way. Their fling was over.

"It'd be nice to keep it as a remembrance of our time together, but we're headed back to reality and my brother right now. I'd like to know where things stand." Her face was colored with a seriousness he hated to see, but he understood why it was there. This was no joke. Zane had crossed a line, and he needed to return to the other side of it.

"I can't betray him, Allison. You know that. Nothing about that has changed." Zane could see the frustration bubbling up inside her. He knew that she was tired of this argument, but it was the truth.

"But the betrayal is done. It happened, and you can't unring that bell. So now the question is what are you going to do about it?"

"You're the one who said we would keep it all between the two of us. I think we stick to the plan. It was amazing, Allison. But it's over." If only the words didn't sound so wrong coming out of his mouth. They certainly weren't enough to convince him. If only they'd had a little more time...to talk all of this through, to share one last mind-melting kiss.

"We're ready to leave," Marcus called for them both from the boat.

Allison stepped past Zane. "Let's just get out of here."

Her tone told him all he needed to know. So that's what last night had been—he'd been an itch that Allison had needed to scratch. Nothing more. He couldn't allow his feelings to be hurt by this revelation. He'd felt that way about many women in the past, and he was certain that women had felt that way about him, as well. Still, it didn't sit entirely right with Zane. Allison had never seemed like the type to love 'em and leave 'em, but her words and her posture were saying exactly that right now.

Between the persistent roar of the wind and the engine noise, Allison and Zane were unable to talk at all on the ride to Eleuthera. As soon as they arrived, a woman who said she was a friend of her aunt Angelique's descended upon them. She was a physician's assistant and insisted on joining them on the Learjet for the flight to Miami. She checked their vital signs and made sure they both ate and drank plenty of water. It was nice to feel taken care of, but at this point, Zane was just ready to get home. Between having weathered the storm, enduring the current cold shoulder from Allison and preparing himself for seeing Scott, Zane was completely and utterly exhausted.

As soon as they landed in Miami and walked into the private terminal, Scott rushed forward and scooped Allison up in her arms. "Thank God you're okay," he said over and over, squeezing her tight.

Zane watched the exchange, remembering the many times Scott had recounted the stories about Allison's cancer as a young girl and the havoc it had wreaked on their entire family. Scott had said many times that he'd never been through anything more difficult than that—life and death, wondering if his sweet and innocent sister would live or die. To hear Scott tell it, every day since then with Allison was regarded as a gift by their entire family.

"I'm fine," she said when he'd finally put her back down on the ground. "Really. Zane took care of me. He made sure nothing happened."

Scott clapped Zane on the shoulder, nodding in appreciation. "I owe you one for keeping her safe."

The guilt Zane had feared was slowly starting to crush him. He'd only done what a good friend would do. But then he'd also done what a good friend *wouldn't* do—he'd slept with his sister. "Honestly, I think she saved me more than the other way around. She would've been just fine on her own. She's too resourceful and smart to get herself into too much trouble." Zane shot her a sideways glance to let her know he had her back. He'd paid attention when they'd talked about this on the island. He understood that she was fighting for Scott to see her in a different light.

"You need to stop worrying so much," Allison said to her brother.

"Plenty of smart people die in natural disasters," Scott said. "Especially when there's flooding."

"She's an unbelievable swimmer. You should have seen her the day we snorkeled over to Mako Island. I could hardly keep up with her. And she wasn't tired at all."

"You two went to Makeout Island?" Scott asked.

Zane wasn't sure he'd heard that right. "Wait? What?"

Scott narrowed his sights on his sister and twisted his lips. "Didn't Allison tell you? That's where teenagers go if they want to hook up with someone and want privacy."

Zane would've laughed if it didn't make the two of them look incredibly guilty. "You told me it was called Mako Island," Zane said to Allison.

"It *is* called that. Scott's being childish." Just then, Allison's phone rang, and she answered it right away. "Hello?" Her face lit up as she listened to what the caller was saying. "Ryan, you are so sweet," she said, distancing herself from her brother and Zane. "I'm totally fine. Just got back to the States. We're in Miami, safe and sound."

Allison's words reverberated in Zane's ears like a bass drum. *Ryan, you are so sweet.* No wonder she'd agreed that anything between them was to stay on the island. There were other men in her orbit, and she didn't want to mess with that. She'd given him an awfully hard time about his unwillingness to get serious with any woman, but she seemed to be playing the field just as hard.

"Hey. Can we talk?" Scott asked Zane.

Zane was not ready to fall under the purview of Scott's eagle eye, especially not when he was so distracted by Allison and her phone call with Ryan. She kept smiling and laughing, which was driving Zane nuts. He was back to not buying the story about working together. "Yeah. Of course."

The pair walked off to a corner of the gate area. Scott stuffed his hands in his pockets and looked down at the floor, seeming tormented. "Is there anything I need to know about? Anything with my sister?"

Zane's brain shifted into overdrive. He did not want to couch things with his best friend, so he was immensely thankful for the phrasing of the question. "There's nothing you need to know about." That much was true. What had happened between Allison and him was entirely private. Nobody's business. She was a grown woman, he was a grown man and they were two adults who had given their enthusiastic consent. End of story.

"You sure?"

"Well, it's been kind of a whirlwind, if that's what you're asking. Not quite the relaxing vacation I'd been hoping for."

"You know that's not what I'm wondering about. I know you. I love you, but there's a damn revolving door in your pants."

Funny, but last night, Zane had been thinking about that very thing, wondering if maybe it wasn't time to set aside his ridiculous bachelor ways. It wasn't making him happy, that was for sure. Those few days he'd spent with Allison were the closest he'd ever felt to having an actual relationship. They'd formed a partnership, they'd worked together and they'd done it well. Plus, being able to act on their incredible chemistry had been a transformative experience. But as Allison hung up her phone and fought a smile, Zane knew that they were back to being nothing more than friends.

"Sorry about that," Allison said, approaching Zane and her brother. The call had been from Ryan Hathaway, who was clearly a great guy. He'd heard about the storm on the news and wanted to make sure she was okay. How sweet was that? She was very excited about the prospect of him interviewing for Black Crescent. "I had to take a work call."

"Yeah. Right," Zane said, his voice clipped. "How's Ryan?"

Oh, hell no. Allison was not going to play this game with Zane, especially when he'd been the one to declare that things were "over" back on the island. "He's wonderful. Thanks for asking. He was really concerned about me and the storm. He wanted to make sure I was safe and sound."

"How nice. He sounds like a great guy." Everything in Zane's tone suggested he did not truly hold this opinion.

Scott looked back and forth between Zane and Allison, seeming perplexed by the conversation. "Uh, okay. I was able to snag the last three first-class seats on the next flight to New Jersey. We'd better get ourselves to the gate. It's boarding in less than an hour."

"What about Allison?" Zane asked, turning his attention to her. "Are you coming with us? I figured you were flying back to LA."

She'd been so nervous about accidentally revealing the Black Crescent information that she hadn't mentioned this detail to Zane. "Didn't I tell you? I'm actually coming back to Falling Brook for a week or so. I have some work I need to do."

"No, you didn't tell me. Do you have a client in town?" Again, his voice was nothing short of perturbed, but Allison was pretty determined to let him stew in his own juices.

"Yes."

"Who is it?"

"I can't say. It's confidential."

"How long is that supposed to last? Falling Brook is not a big place, and I have lived there my entire life. I'm going to find out sooner or later."

Allison's pulse raced. She felt queasy at the thought of Zane figuring this out. She knew exactly how he would react—badly. "If you were my client, I wouldn't talk about you to anyone else. It's just the right thing to do."

He rolled his damn eyes, not bothering to say that of course it made sense for her to keep things to herself for the sake of her business interests. She could hardly believe how things between her and Zane had changed in the last few hours. So much for fantasies brought to life—she wondered now if it wouldn't have been better to keep Zane in her dreams, rather than begging him to become a reality. *Careful what you wish for.* It hurt too much to have him be such a jerk to her. And to think that she'd been mulling over some ridiculous confessions last night when she couldn't fall asleep. She'd wanted to tell him that she wanted more of him. So much more. And if he'd given her any indication that he might feel the same way, she would have been all in. She would have even called Kianna and told her that they had to drop Black Crescent.

The Allison of last night was clearly an idiot. It didn't matter that she and Zane had had an amazing time on the island together, and not just in bed. It didn't matter that he'd made her happy. Made her laugh. Made her feel sexy and desired. Zane would always choose his friendship with Scott over her, and she couldn't entirely blame him. That relationship had longevity. It had never faltered. He could count on it, and Allison understood how anyone would want to stick to the things in life that were reliable, especially if you were Zane, a man who'd been through the wringer.

That still didn't keep her from wanting him.

The three of them took a shuttle over to the commercial terminal and waited to board, standing on the concourse outside the busy gate area. Scott and Zane had been knee-deep in conversation, leaving Allison to feel like the third wheel until Zane wandered off to find a bathroom and Scott pulled Allison aside.

"You didn't tell him why you were coming back to Falling Brook?" Scott asked her pointedly.

"Wow. You really don't waste any time, don't you?"

"It's a valid question, and he's going to be back any minute now. You two just rode out the storm together and the topic of you coming back to Falling Brook never came up? Not once? It makes me wonder what in the heck you two did talk about."

"I don't want him to know about Black Crescent, okay? And I don't want you to tell him, either. You know how he feels about it. You know it hurts him to talk or hear about it, and you also know he has a blind spot when it comes to the Lowells. I don't want it to mess with our friendship."

"Since when have you two been close?"

If Allison could've shot laser beams from her eyes at her brother, she would have. Why did he have to think that only he could be close to Zane? "We've always been friends, Scott. You know that. I can't compete with your friendship, okay? So don't try to compare the two." She saw down the concourse that Zane was on his way back already. Even in rumpled clothes, with two days of scruff on his face and with an attitude that was decidedly cooler than the one she'd experienced during their last day on the island, he was irresistible. She was going to have to learn to resist. "He and I just went through a life-and-death situation, and I don't want to hurt his feelings unnecessarily. He's tired. I'm tired. Plus, there's a good chance that I won't get hired by BC long term. So if it's only a one-off, I really don't see the point in telling him and hurting his feelings for no good reason."

Scott nodded. "Okay. That's probably the right call then. Your intentions are good."

Zane smiled as he approached them. It still made Allison's heart melt. She was going to have to figure out a way to get over him. She had no idea how that would work. "You guys talking about me?" he asked.

"Always," Scott said.

"Never," Allison countered.

"Ladies and gentlemen," the gate agent announced over the intercom. "We're ready to begin the boarding process for Flight 1506 with nonstop service to Newark International Airport. We'll begin by inviting our first-class passengers to board."

"That's us," Scott said.

"Good. I can't wait to get home to a hot shower and a good night's sleep," Zane said.

Allison felt the same way. She also wished she could do those things with Zane. She was going to need to work up to this whole business of forgetting her attraction to him.

The three boarded the plane, but as soon as Allison figured out the seating arrangement, she realized just how much she would always be the odd man out when it came to her brother and Zane. The two guys were seated together, across the aisle from her. That had been Scott's decision, since he'd booked the flights, and Zane was obviously perfectly happy with it. Allison flagged the flight attendant and asked for a gin and tonic before takeoff. She needed something to soothe her ragged edges. Maybe she could catch some sleep after they were in the air.

But for now, since Zane and Scott were immersed in conversation, and the plane was still boarding, Allison took this chance to give Kianna a quick call.

"Tell me you're okay," she blurted without even saying hello.

"I'm fine. In one piece. On the plane to New Jersey."

"I can't believe that storm hit the island. It all happened so fast. I kept watching the forecast, hoping it would change for you. I can't help but feel responsible. It was my idea for you to go down there in the first place."

"No. No. It's not your fault. I wanted to go. And believe it or not, it was still a good trip. Despite the storm. Despite everything." She was trying to put the best possible spin on this, not merely for Kianna's sake, but also for her own. She didn't want to regret her time with Zane. She didn't want to believe that it might have been a big mistake. But what do you do when you get what you've always wanted and then it's snatched away by timing and circumstance? What do you do when the guy you've wanted for years tells you that it's over before it's had a chance to really start? Right now, it felt like nothing would ever sting as much as this rejection.

"Did you at least find a hot guy? Please say yes."

Allison couldn't suppress the smile that crossed her face. "I did. But I'll have to tell you about it later. We take off soon, and I have to turn off my phone."

"Okay, hon. Did you postpone your meeting with Black Crescent?"

"Nope. Still going in tomorrow. As planned."

"Did you talk to Joshua Lowell?"

"I texted his assistant. We're all good."

"You're a badass, you know that, right?"

Allison laughed. Her friendship and partnership with Kianna meant the world to her. She really hoped she wouldn't end up letting her down. This Black Crescent meeting had to go well. "I'm trying."

"Call me after the meeting tomorrow?"

"You know it. Talk to you then."

Allison hung up the phone, switched it to airplane mode and tucked it into the seat-back pocket. She swirled her gin and tonic, took a long sip and glanced over at Zane and Scott. Zane, who was sitting at the window, made eye contact with her. That instant seemed to speak volumes—there was a connection between them that hadn't been there before they got to the island. Zane knew it. She did, too. But he seemed resigned to setting it aside. Keeping it in the past. No matter how hot and passionate that connection was, it didn't seem to be enough for Zane.

He dropped his gaze and returned his attention to her brother. Allison's heart plummeted to her stomach, but she was used to the disappointment now.

It was the story of her life with Zane. And exactly the reason why this visit to Falling Brook would be all about her role as businessperson supreme, not the woman who couldn't stop pining for a man she couldn't have.

Scott leaned across the aisle to talk to her. "Do you have plans tomorrow night?"

"Hanging out at your house. Not sure what else I would possibly be doing."

"I wasn't sure if you had work obligations."

Allison wanted to strangle her brother for bringing up Black Crescent while Zane was sitting right next to him. "Nope. I should be done by midafternoon. Why?"

Zane peered around Scott. "He invited me over for dinner."

"I wanted to thank him for taking such good care of my little sister," Scott added.

What in the world was her brother up to? "Okay. Sounds great."

Nine

Right on time, Allison pulled her rental car into the Black Crescent parking lot the following afternoon, shortly before two o'clock. She'd arrived back in Falling Brook in the nick of time—less than twenty-four hours before her scheduled meeting with Haley Shaw and Joshua Lowell. Anyone else might have used the fact that she'd been stranded on an island in the middle of a hurricane as an excuse to postpone the meeting, but that detail was a dramatic selling point. She could tell Josh Lowell that not even a natural disaster would keep her from doing her job, and doing it well. In the end, she and Kianna needed the Black Crescent contract. It was their best shot at keeping their company alive.

Of course, the only trouble with that was Zane. If she got the contract, she would have to tell him that she was working for the company that he considered the enemy. Even though there were no more remnants of romance between them, she couldn't keep the secret from him forever. As she walked up to the sleek and modern building that had always stuck out in the otherwise traditional Falling Brook landscape, she was well aware that if Zane knew what she was doing right now, he would tell her she was not only a terrible friend, she was foolish. The things he'd said while they were riding out the storm in the Bahamas echoed in her head. *The Lowells destroy everything. Families most of all.* He'd been deeply hurt by the things the Lowell family had done to him and his parents, and it was clear that for Zane, it was about far more than the money. His entire world was turned upside down the day that Vernon Lowell made off with his family's fortune. As far as Zane was concerned, his old charmed life ended that day and his new, far less shiny life began.

Allison had a somewhat different perspective. Oddly enough, she felt a debt of gratitude to the Lowells. If Vernon hadn't disappeared with all that money, she might have never met Zane. That thinking might be employing some pretty messed-up logic, but that was truly the way she felt. Not having Zane in her life was an incredibly depressing thought, almost as sad as the other thought that had

been winding through her head since the Bahamas—
that Zane would ultimately be a thirst unquenched.
She'd thought that making love with him would get
him out of her system. But that had been a horrible
miscalculation on her part.

The flight had given her entirely too much time
to mull over Zane's latest rejection. She wanted
to shrug it off and move ahead, but her heart just
wouldn't let her go there. Her heart wanted to drag
her down to the bottom of this murky sea in which
she was adrift and remind her of the reasons why it
was such a shattering disappointment to have him
choose his friendship with her brother over a chance
with her. She was in deep, and she had no idea how
to swim her way out. Scott would never buy into
the idea of her with Zane. He would always think
of Allison as that little girl with cancer, even when
she was strong and healthy and a grown woman.
And if anyone knew Zane forward, backward and
every other way imaginable, it was her brother. He
was convinced that Zane wasn't capable of commitment. The allure of other women was too great, although Allison also suspected that there was more
to it than that. Zane might have been unbelievably
brave in the face of that storm, but he was afraid of
commitment and was possibly even more terrified
of love. That put Allison in the category of a good
time, right where every other woman he'd ever met

also resided. Allison didn't want to be just another girl, but it sure felt that way.

With the Black Crescent building looming before her, Allison couldn't afford to think about that. She had a job to do and a business to keep afloat. Her first allegiance had to be to herself and Kianna now. She straightened her designer jacket and shrugged her laptop bag up onto her shoulder, then marched into Black Crescent.

She approached the main-floor reception desk. "Allison Randall for Joshua Lowell. We have a two o'clock."

The receptionist picked up the phone. "One moment, please."

Before she could dial an extension number, another woman emerged from a side door in the reception area. "Ms. Randall?" The woman was willowy with wavy blond hair. She offered her hand. "I'm Halcy Shaw, Mr. Lowell's assistant. We're so glad you're here. Especially considering everything you've been through. I still can't believe you were able to keep this appointment."

Allison shook hands with Haley. "It would've taken more than some bad weather to keep me away from this opportunity."

"Come on. I'll give you the lay of the land and show you where we'll be conducting the interviews."

Haley led Allison upstairs to the second floor and a conference room right outside Joshua Lowell's office.

The one thing that struck Allison about Black Crescent was that no expense had been spared. Every detail was of the finest quality. It did make Allison wonder if the rumors about Vernon Lowell were true, that he'd never actually left Falling Brook and had merely been in hiding this whole time. If that was ever proved to be the case, she could imagine Zane blowing his top. Another lie from Vernon Lowell would only reopen Zane's deep wounds. Plus, Zane was the sort of the man who wanted to get even. Knowing he could have hunted down Vernon all these years would at the very least eat at him.

"Please, make yourself at home," Haley said, gesturing to the gleaming mahogany meeting table. "Mr. Lowell should be here in a few minutes. He's just finishing up a phone call."

Allison set down her Louis Vuitton bag and pulled out her laptop. "Great. We're seeing three candidates today. Ryan Hathaway, Chase Hargrove and Matteo Velez."

Haley pursed her lips in a particularly odd way. "Chase Hargrove, huh?" Her voice was dripping with doubt, something Allison wanted to get to the bottom of before Joshua arrived.

"Yes. He's highly qualified for the position. And I was impressed with him when we spoke on the phone."

Haley nodded, but seemed unconvinced. "I'm sure

he has the right credentials. I just don't know if he's a good fit for the office."

This was an interesting development. Allison had never had an assistant offer her opinion of a candidate, and especially not before the interview had even taken place. But in her experience assistants seemed to always know more about everyone and everything than the majority of their bosses. "Can you tell me why?"

Just then, a young man poked his head into the meeting room. "Ms. Shaw. Chase Hargrove is here for his interview."

"Can you let Mr. Lowell know? And can you ask Chase to hold on a minute?" Haley asked.

"Sure thing, Ms. Shaw." The man darted back into the hall.

"If there's something I need to know, now would be a great time to mention it," Allison said. She couldn't afford to mess up when it came to Black Crescent. She had to nail this job. On paper, Chase was a highly qualified candidate, and Allison had found him charming and affable during their one phone conversation.

Haley seemed deep in thought for a moment, as if she was calculating her response. "I'm afraid I don't have a specific reason for feeling that way about Chase. It's more of a hunch."

The meeting door opened again and in walked Joshua Lowell. Allison had never met him in person, but she'd seen his pictures all over the papers and in business magazines, especially the last few years. "Mr. Lowell, I'm Allison Randall." She offered her hand.

"Please. Call me Joshua. It won't be long before I'm not the boss around here anymore."

"That's why I'm here, right?" Allison wondered if that aspect of her job might help her smooth things over with Zane whenever he discovered she was working for Black Crescent. So much of his hatred seemed aimed at Joshua, and she was in charge of finding his replacement. She tucked the idea away in her head. The idea of needing to explain herself to Zane, all in the name of making a case for them as a couple, was a stretch. She was sure he didn't see her as anything more than a fling.

"Absolutely," Joshua answered. "So, please, let's bring in these candidates."

Allison asked Haley to go ahead and bring Chase in for his interview. The instant he walked through the door, the energy in the room changed dramatically. Tall, handsome and completely self-assured, Chase was a formidable presence. With Joshua also in the room, it was no easy task to take center stage, but Chase seemed to do it at will. Was this the reason for Haley's hesitancy when it came to Chase? Was he simply too much to deal with?

Chase sat opposite the three of them at the conference table and Allison wasted no time conducting the interview. This was not about putting the candidate on the spot—she'd already gone over these exact questions with them over the phone. They'd also already been fully vetted by Allison and Kianna. This process was all for the client. This was Chase's chance to put his well-honed answers on full display for Joshua.

When Allison was finished, she was fairly certain Chase could not only land the job, but could perform the duties with aplomb. But she wasn't done with showing off the product of her hard work—Ryan Hathaway and Matteo Velez were up next.

"Thank you so much, Chase, for coming in today. We'll be in touch," Allison said.

All four of them stood and Chase began to round the table.

"I'll fetch Mr Hathaway," Haley blurted, darting out the door before Chase had a chance to shake her hand and say goodbye.

Chase took notice, watching as she disappeared. "Ms. Shaw sure is on the case, isn't she?"

Joshua extended his hand to Chase. "She's the best. No matter who comes in as CEO, Haley needs to stay. She makes this office run."

"Believe me, if I get this job, Ms. Shaw is the last person I'd dream of replacing," Chase said. Allison couldn't ignore the glimmer in his eyes.

Just then, Haley walked in with Ryan Hathaway, who Allison recognized from his headshot. Typically,

Allison did not want the candidates for a position to encounter each other in the interview room, but what was done was done. She made the introductions, and Ryan seemed immediately suspicious of Chase.

"I suppose this is my cue to make way for your interview," Chase said to Ryan before turning to Haley. "And, Ms. Shaw, I hope to see you again very soon."

Haley's face flushed with a brilliant shade of pink. She was noticeably conflicted as they shook hands. "I wish you the best of luck."

Ryan seemed to take notice of the sparks between Haley and Chase, arching both eyebrows and pressing his lips together firmly as he witnessed their goodbye. He pulled Allison aside as Haley and Joshua talked privately.

"Is there something I need to know about that guy? Did he already get the job? I don't want to interview for a taken position," he said.

Allison shook her head, but she could tell that Ryan was seriously concerned. Given their earlier conversations, she was eager to put him at ease. "Everything's fine. I think he's just a little heavy-handed with the charm. If I had to place a bet on it, I'd say he has a bit of a crush on Ms. Shaw."

Ryan glanced over his shoulder. Joshua and Haley were still conferring. "Okay. Good."

Allison gently placed her hand on Ryan's shoulder. "You sure you're okay?"

He nodded enthusiastically. "Yes. Definitely. I'm

just used to guys like that being rewarded for their bad behavior. You know what they say. Nice guys finish last."

Allison took a moment to consider Ryan's words. Had he been burned? Was that where that was coming from? If so, she felt his pain. She'd gone for what she wanted, and it had been a miserable fail. "Nice guys finish first with me. As long as they're qualified and nail the interview, of course."

Ryan grinned. "I'm glad you recruited me. I really enjoyed our conversation while you were on your trip. I'm so relieved you weren't hurt in the storm. Everything I saw on the news looked terrifying."

"It wasn't fun, that's for sure." Except that it had been. It had been amazing. She'd never felt more alive when the sea seemed determined to carry them away, but Zane was resolute about keeping her safe. She'd let herself be vulnerable with him, something she rarely ever did, and in the moment, it had been so richly rewarding. Even with Zane behaving like an ass since then, and trying to discount everything that had happened between them, she knew in her heart that it had all been worth it. Kissing him, touching him, having his hands all over her body. She'd wanted him for so long. How could she have ever said no? Even if she'd known all along what would happen? She couldn't have.

Allison shook her head and brought herself back to the present. She couldn't daydream about Zane right now. Not with work on the line. "I have to ask if you're looking at other positions right now," she said to Ryan.

"I have a few more interviews over the next several weeks. But I'll be honest. This is the job I really want."

There was no greater satisfaction than finding the right candidate for the job, and Allison had a good feeling about Ryan. "Music to my ears. Now, let's see if Mr. Lowell and Ms. Shaw are ready to get this show on the road."

Ryan hit it out of the park during his interview, as did Matteo after him. When it was time to say goodbye to Josh and Haley, Allison knew she'd done an amazing job.

"Very impressive, Ms. Randall," Joshua said, sitting back in his chair. "Thank you for going the extra mile in making today happen."

"Literally," Haley added. "She just flew back from the Bahamas last night."

"I'll do whatever it takes to make my clients happy." Allison collected her papers into a neat stack. "Do you have a sense of the timeline for the hire?"

"I'm eager to get the new CEO in as soon as possible. What are your thoughts as far as the timing for second interviews?"

"It'll depend on the candidates' schedules and yours, of course, but Haley and I can coordinate. I do recommend you think about it for at least a week.

Spend some time with the files and background info I provided. In my experience, it's best to not rush with a decision like this."

Joshua nodded, seeming to consider all she said. "I suppose you're right. I'm just ready to move forward."

Allison couldn't help but think of the subtext—he was eager to move on with his life. He had love and happiness ahead, and he didn't want to wait. "Of course. I understand."

"Will you be able to stay in Falling Brook for a few weeks? It would be great if I knew I could call on you to walk us through this process. The phone is one thing, but there's no substitute for having some-one on hand."

Allison knew this was her opening for driving home the deal she wanted to make. "It depends on whether or not I'm on retainer. I have a partner out in Los Angeles and other clients who also expect my time."

"I'll pay triple your normal retainer for the next month." Joshua hadn't hesitated to up the ante. "That should give us enough time to make a hire for this position."

Allison swallowed hard. Three times her nor-mal rate was certainly a great starting point. "And beyond that?"

"The new CEO will ultimately make the call as to whether we put you on permanent retainer. But I will certainly have a say in it, and, as far as I'm concerned, you have the job."

Goose bumps raced over the surface of Allison's skin. Any sliver of victory in business felt good, and Kianna was going to flip out when she got the good news. Even so, there was a downside. A month in Falling Brook would make it impossible to stay away from Zane. And that meant she had to come clean with him about working with Black Crescent. "Fantastic. I'm staying with my brother here in Falling Brook, working out of his house. I can be on-site anytime you need me. Just call."

"You can expect to hear from me."

Allison strode out of the meeting, feeling as though she was walking on a cloud. She'd nailed it, in every sense of the term. She called Kianna and told her everything as soon as she got in the car.

"You are not only a badass, you're a rock star," Kianna said.

"It's only a month. It's not the long-term retainer we wanted."

"It'll come. I know you'll get it done."

"I'll do my best."

"So, can you tell me about the guy in the Bahamas?"

Allison hesitated, not sure she wanted to dive into the topic. This wasn't a quick conversation, and there was so much about this situation that she was still trying to mentally unpack. "His name is Zane. I've known him for fifteen years. He's a friend of my brother's, and we just happened to end up at Rose Cove at the same time." She decided to skip the heavier part of the story, the details about how she'd been longing for him all those years and that the idea of letting go was a miserable one.

"Did he at least rock your world?"

"Oh, yes. Several times."

"And now?"

"I don't know. I think we're back to just being friends."

"Are you happy with that arrangement?"

Allison sighed. She wasn't happy with it, but she also didn't see a way past it. Maybe it really was easier if she and Zane stayed friends. "I'm not sure, but I'll figure out at least some of it tonight. He's coming over to my brother's for dinner."

Ten

Zane's first day back at the office after the Bahamas trip was less than productive. Between a million phone calls from concerned friends and clients, and his pervasive thoughts of Allison, he got very little work done. For some ridiculous reason, he kept seeing flashes of Allison flitting around the island in her sarong. It was so bad that he'd referred to one of his marketing managers as Allison when her name was in fact Maria. He hadn't even been close. A mistake easily swept aside when he blamed it on the exhaustion from the storm, but it was a sign that he was going to have deal with this. It had been short-sighted to think that he and Allison could sleep together, shrug it off and return to their old dynamic. So where would they land? He had no idea.

By the time he'd hopped in his BMW to head to Scott's house for dinner, he was still catching up. He'd left a voice mail for his mom, but she was just now calling him back. He pressed the button to put her on speaker.

"Hi, Mom. I take it you got my message?"

"I didn't even know you'd left the country. Shows you how out of the loop I am."

"Would it have been better if I'd told you I was down there? Wouldn't you have worried? I know you don't like to worry."

"Well, of course, I would've been concerned, but you're a survivor, Zane. I never doubt your ability to figure out how to find your way through a tough situation."

The undertone of her comment was that he'd managed just fine in his teenage years when everything had gone south. It was nice to get that stamp of approval, although he knew that it was just his mother being a mom. "Thanks."

"What took you down there? New marketing client in the Bahamas?"

"I went on vacation."

"No!" His mother gasped, which turned into her musical laugh. "My son? Went away for fun?"

Zane had to chuckle, too. "Believe it or not, yes.

I've been stressed, and I needed to get out of Falling Brook to clear my head."

"Are things at work not going well?"

Zane took the turn onto Scott's street. Scott and his wife lived in one of the original Falling Brook neighborhoods, which was seeing a revival. Older, stately homes were being remodeled and updated, with young families moving in. Zane saw it as a move in the right direction. This town needed some freshening up. "Actually, things at work are amazing. We're too busy, but in a good way. We've reached the point where we're turning away potential clients. That's something I never even imagined six or seven years ago."

"Then what's bothering you?"

Zane pulled up in front of Scott's house, a recently restored five-bedroom Tudor with a pristine putting green of a front yard that was Scott's pride and joy. Zane put the car in Park and killed the engine, sitting back in the driver's seat and running his hand through his hair.

"You're being quiet," his mom said. "Just come out with it. You know you can tell me anything."

He knew that. It didn't make his embarrassment over what he was about to say any less real. "It's Joshua Lowell. I got sucked into some drama with him. Someone anonymously sent me a paternity test saying that he had a child he wasn't willing to claim responsibility for. I talked to a local reporter who was working on a piece about him."

"Have you lost your mind? Why would you get involved in that?"

"I don't know. Revenge? Or as close as I'll ever get to it? It doesn't really matter now. It all backfired. The story ran, without that bombshell, and Josh Lowell ended up smelling like a rose, he and the reporter fell in love and now he's getting married. He's even leaving Black Crescent."

She sighed heavily.

"I know," Zane said. "The guy is golden. Everything he does turns out perfectly, and it makes me nuts. I know it shouldn't, but it does. Just thinking about it is making my shoulders lock up." He cranked his head from side to side, hoping to loosen the tension.

"You realize that people think the same thing about you. That you're golden. That you can do no wrong."

"*You* might say that about me, but other people do not. Plus, that isn't the point."

"But it *is* the point. It's not just me who says it, either. Your father thinks the same thing. Your grandparents. Aunts and uncles. Your colleagues and employees. Remember when you invited me to your company Christmas party two years ago? All night long, all I heard about was how great you are and it's not just because you're the boss. I heard it from your clients, as well. I'm your mom, and even I got a little sick of it."

Zane laughed, but he was astonished to be hearing this from her. He'd never seen himself as anything more than the guy who was still striving to get back on top.

"Look at your life," she continued. "You have an immensely successful business. You own a beautiful home in one of the most exclusive towns in the country. You're handsome, and people love you. Whatever it is that you think the Lowells stole from us or from you, it doesn't matter. It hasn't kept you from having it all, and it never will keep you from it. You need to find a way to move forward."

"This isn't just about what they did to me. It's about what they did to our family. The Lowells are the reason you and dad split up."

"You know, your dad and I had a drink a few weeks ago. We talked about it."

"You did?" His parents' divorce had been as acrimonious as they came. To Zane's knowledge, his parents had only been in the same place twice since their split fourteen years ago, at Zane's high school and college graduations, and they'd barely spoken to each other. "You didn't tell me this."

"He came to Boston for work, and he called me. It was nice. We had a chance to say a lot of things that should've been said a long time ago. The truth is that your dad and I were never going to make it. Of course, losing everything put a massive strain on the marriage, but the underlying problems were already there. We weren't in love. I'm not sure we ever were. We would have split up eventually."

Zane was struggling to keep up, but he couldn't help but notice that it felt as if a weight was being lifted. A burden from his past was evaporating before his eyes. "Wow, Mom. You are kind of blowing my mind right now."

"Does that help you see that you need to let Joshua Lowell do his own thing and maybe get out there and keep looking for your own happiness? You know, I'd like to have a daughter-in-law, maybe become a grandmother at some point."

"Mom…"

"No pressure."

"Oh, right. No pressure." Zane glanced at the clock on his dashboard. It was seven o'clock and he didn't want to be late. "Mom, I need to run. Scott invited me over for dinner and I'm sitting outside his house. His sister, Allison, is in town."

"Oh, how nice. Say hi to them both for me. I've always adored those two, especially Allison. She's always been such a sweetheart to me."

And just like that, Zane felt like the universe might be telling him to salvage the romance that had started at Rose Cove. It was at least worth trying. "Love you, Mom."

"Love you, too."

Zane grabbed the bottle of Chateau Musar he'd brought, which was Scott's favorite wine, and hopped out of the car. He strode up the long driveway and couldn't ignore the way his pulse picked up at the thought of seeing Allison again. Maybe this could actually work. Of course, there was a lot standing in his way. He'd have to find a way to sort things out with Scott. And he'd have to hope that there weren't other guys in the mix. He'd also have to smooth Allison's ruffled feathers. He'd been a jerk when they left the island. Allison deserved so much better than that. As to how difficult it would be to convince her to accept his apology, he wasn't sure. He was prepared to grovel. It was difficult for him to set aside his pride, but he'd overcome worse.

He rang the doorbell, and Scott quickly answered, waving him in. When Zane handed over the wine, Scott unleashed a mile-wide grin. "You're the best friend a guy can have. Let's get this decanted."

Zane followed him inside. He was looking forward to spending an evening with these people he cared about so deeply, but coming to dinner at Scott's house felt a bit like returning to the scene of the crime, given the kiss with Allison at his birthday party. He wished he could find a way to rewind the clock to that moment when her luscious lips first met his. If only he'd known then that she hadn't done it on a lark. She'd spent years building up to it.

They wound their way down the wide central

entry and into the newly remodeled gourmet kitchen. Scott's wife, Brittney, was cutting up vegetables at the center island. "Look who's here," she said, taking a kiss on the cheek from Zane. "I'm glad you could come over on such short notice. Scott was eager to express his thanks."

"He keeps saying that, but Allison would've been fine without me. Seriously. She's tough as nails."

She swept the contents of the cutting board into a large bowl. "I agree. But you know how he is. Super protective. Is there such a thing as a helicopter brother?"

"Hey. I'm standing right here." Scott sniffed the wine cork, then emptied the bottle into a decanter.

"Well, the kids and I are thankful if nothing else," Brittney said. "I swear the only thing that kept Scott from freaking out about Allison was knowing that you were down there with her."

"Did I hear my name?" Allison poked her head into the kitchen.

Zane's heart did a veritable flip when he saw her. There had been countless moments on the island when he'd been taken aback by her beauty, but right now, with her sun-kissed skin glowing and the stress of their life-and-death situation during the storm no longer showing its effects, she absolutely stole his breath away. "There she is."

Allison grabbed at the kitchen counter and dragged one leg into the kitchen, followed by the other. Zane peeked around the island and saw what was slowing her down—Scott's five-year-old daughter, Lily, had wrapped herself around Allison's ankle. "Sorry. I'm having some trouble walking today," Allison said. She gave her eyebrows a conspiratorial bounce.

"I noticed there's a large growth on your leg. I'd better take a look at it and make sure it's not anything contagious." He crouched down and looked Lily in the eye. The little girl was already giggling. "I might need to administer the tickle test."

"Noooo!" Lily unspooled herself from Allison's leg, rolled across the floor and scrambled off behind her mother.

"Miss Thing," Brittney said. "You and Franklin need to go get washed up for dinner."

"Can we eat in front of the TV?" Lily asked, warily peering at Zane.

"Yes. I think the grown-ups would enjoy some adult conversation anyway."

Scott scooped up Lily into his arms. "Come on. Let's go hunt down your brother."

Brittney nodded to two empty wineglasses on the kitchen counter. "Why don't you two grab a drink for yourselves? We'll be ready to eat in a little bit."

"You sure we can't help?" Allison asked.

"I'm sure. Cooking is one of the only things that relax me," Brittney said.

"Wine?" Zane glanced at Allison, wondering how

she was feeling about being around him. She had every reason in the world to give him some steely attitude. And he was going to have to find a way to work through it. "We can go out on the balcony and catch up."

"About what? Not much has happened since yesterday."

He knew then that he was going to have to try a little harder. "You can tell me how your meeting with your client went."

Allison found it impossible to swallow and not much easier to breathe. Zane had picked the one topic of conversation she did not want to explore, especially not when he was looking good enough to eat. Damn him. It was one thing when he was wearing a pair of board shorts, but there was something about Zane in a pair of perfectly tailored flat-front trousers and a dress shirt, with the sleeves rolled up to the elbows, that absolutely slayed her. He would always have her number. Even when he'd been a jerk to her. Even when he was going around picking uncomfortable things to discuss. "Wine sounds great, but I'd rather skip work talk. It's been a long day."

"Whatever you want."

He poured them each a glass of wine, and she tried to ignore the pull he had on her. It came from the vicinity of her belly button, although just being around him made the more feminine parts of her body quake and yearn, as well. They stepped out onto the patio overlooking the back of Scott and Brittney's beautiful wooded lot. The early-evening air was warm and breezy, hearkening back to their time on the island. Part of her wanted to go back so badly and relive every unbelievable minute, but she knew that wasn't reality, and one thing she prided herself on, aside from her predilection for fantasies about Zane, was her ability to stay grounded.

"Did you sleep well last night?" He took a sip of his wine after he posed the question, regarding her with a look that took no effort from him and still felt like pure seduction.

"Like the proverbial rock."

"We didn't get much sleep during that last day or so on the island, did we?" He leaned against the balcony railing, inexplicably turning her on by leaving his firm forearms on display.

She smiled. Heat rushed to her face. "No, we did not. That damn storm kept us up."

A subtle blush colored his cheeks, and he hung his head, nodding. "Right. It was the storm that kept us awake. The weather was nothing if not distracting."

She sucked in a deep breath. She loved this glimmer of normalcy between them, their ability to fall into a fun back-and-forth, but it only made her crave more. Was there a way to get beyond the things standing between them? Even if Scott was ever able to get over himself, the Black Crescent problem was inescapable. Her meeting had gone exceptionally well today. She wasn't about to turn her back on hard-earned success, no matter how much she knew it would anger Zane. Yes, she would come clean, but everything else was on Zane. It was his choice. Not hers.

She glanced over her shoulder to make sure Scott or Brittney wasn't looking. "No matter what, I will never regret what happened, Zane. I need you to know that. It was amazing."

He straightened to his full height, leaving her in the shadow of his towering frame, and touched her arm gently. How could he bring her entire body to life with only an instant of caring contact? "Yes. Of course. I feel the same way."

Her heart began to gallop in her chest, beating an uneven rhythm.

"Dinner's ready." Scott was standing at the door to the balcony. His vision noticeably landed on Zane's hand touching Allison's arm.

Allison reflexively pulled back from Zane, and he did the same. The instant it happened, a wave of guilt blanketed her. Resentment followed. These games were so stupid. And idiotic. She had to put an end to them. Part of that was finding the right time to tell Zane about Black Crescent. "On our way."

Allison and Zane joined Scott and Brittney in the dining room. On the front of the house, it had a splendid view of the front yard, and was appointed with all of the elegant trappings of a comfortable life. Allison didn't like to get too wrapped up in material things. There was plenty of that going on in LA. Still, she could admit that she wanted this for herself. She wanted a husband and a house and children. More to the point, she wanted love and a life partner. She wanted it all.

The spread Brittney put out was truly spectacular— filet mignon cooked to an ideal medium-rare, with rosemary roasted baby potatoes and green beans. The wine Zane had brought was a sublime complement to the meal, and Scott seemed nothing if not relaxed and content because of it. The conversation was fun and light, full of laughs and interesting stories. Zane and Scott told tales—a few from high school, but most from recent years, stories about pickup basketball, epic golf tournaments and even a few nights out drinking. All Allison could think as she watched Zane and Scott together was that she didn't merely appreciate that they had such a solid friendship, but that she also loved being witness to it. It was a real shame that Zane was a no-go because he was her brother's best friend. In a lot of ways, it was also what made him perfect.

There were a few moments when Zane delivered a knowing glance with his piercing gaze, leaving Allison to grapple with the resulting hum in her body. Did he know that he could affect her like that without so much as a brush of a finger against the back of her hand? Did he know how much it made her want him, and how frustrating it made the knowledge that she'd never likely experience his touch again?

At the end of the meal, the conversation continued in the kitchen as the four of them cleaned up. They were just about finished when Lily walked in, complaining of a stomachache.

"Come on, sweetheart," Brittney said. "It's probably time for you to go to bed anyway. Why don't you say good-night to Aunt Allison and Uncle Zane?"

Lily merely waved at them, curling into her mom's hip. "Good night."

Allison crouched down to give Lily a kiss on the forehead. "Sweet dreams, Lils."

"Good night."

"I'm going to help Brittney with bedtime. I'll be back in a few minutes," Scott said.

The quiet in the kitchen when her brother left was deafening. She and Zane had just been presented with the same scenario they'd been in last month. Except this time, the playing field had definitely changed. Gone were many of Allison's old reservations, replaced by newer and more intense ones. She didn't have to wonder how badly it hurt to be rejected by Zane. She'd experienced it firsthand.

"I forgot you were staying here." Zane took a step closer to her.

"Yes. I always do. The guest room is beautiful. Very comfortable." She leaned back against the kitchen island, gripping the cool marble counter with both hands.

"Good bed?" he asked.

She laughed and shook her head. "Smooth, Zane. Real smooth."

He shrugged and inched even closer. "I had an opening, I had to take it." His hand was inches from hers. He reached out with his thumb and lightly caressed her fingers.

A zip of electricity wound its way down her spine. "Zane..."

"Yes? That is my name." He slipped his fingers under her hand and lifted it to his lips. It made her dizzy.

"My brother."

"His name is Scott. And he's in the other room. And we're here. And I've missed you." He kissed her hand again, except this time, he closed his eyes and seemed to savor it.

She nearly passed out, but she had to keep her head straight. "You're being so goofy. You missed me? I just saw you yesterday."

He opened his eyes. "I know. And I was an ass by the dock."

Hard to believe that had only been thirty-six hours ago. It felt like a lifetime. "Yes, you were. I get it, but it doesn't change the fact that I wasn't a fan."

Scott's voice came from the hall.

"Come on. Let's get out of here." Zane tugged on her hand.

"What? Now? Where?" Her vision darted to the kitchen entry, then back to Zane.

He rolled his eyes. "So many questions." He pulled her back into the dining room, where they could buy a few more seconds of privacy. "Come to my place, Allison. I want to be alone with you. I need to be alone with you."

Her pulse went to thundering in her body the way it had during the storm. "What about what you said to me at the dock?"

"I was an idiot. I'm sorry."

"There's more to it, and you know that. What about Scott?"

"Now you sound like me." He again raised her hand to his lips and delivered a soul-bending kiss. "No more excuses. Let's get out of here, spend some time together and we'll deal with him later. I need to be alone with you, Allison."

How in the hell could she say no to that? She couldn't, even when there was a small part of her that wanted to press him for more. For an explanation. For clarification about everything. But the reality was that she'd been waiting forever to hear him saying something so desperate, especially unprompted. So she'd take Zane's offer. Even if it ended up being only sex. One more time. "What do we tell Scott?"

Zane pulled his phone out of his pocket and

tapped away at the screen. He showed it to her. Taking your sister for a drive. Thanks for dinner.

"That's it?" she asked.

"That's it." He tapped at his screen one more time, took her hand and out the door they went.

Just like Allison had always wanted.

Eleven

This was crazy. Absolutely certifiable. But something about the impetuousness of stealing away from her brother's house with Zane, like a couple of brazen teenagers, made it so thrilling. Perhaps it was because at this time yesterday, when they'd been on the plane back to New Jersey, she'd been convinced this was never going to happen again. It might be foolish and stupid, but she had a glimmer of optimism. She hoped like hell Zane wouldn't end up quashing it again. If he did, the disappointment would be of her making. She'd said yes to this. She'd gone with him because her heart had convinced her to take another chance.

Zane was showing off with the car, taking turns a

little too fast, changing lanes when he had a whisper-thin margin of error and generally acting as though he didn't care about repercussions. Allison sat back in the seat and allowed him his macho moment while she studied his grip on the steering wheel and counted the seconds until they would be at his place and those glorious hands of his could be all over her naked body.

The trip probably clocked in at under twenty minutes, but all of that anticipation made it feel as though it had been a cross-country trek. She'd never been to Zane's place before, which was in one of the newest and most exclusive neighborhoods in town. The street was lined with stately houses, but Allison found Zane's to be the most beautiful. Tucked away on top of a hill, a long stone driveway leading to it, the sprawling home was an oasis in this bustling town. She couldn't help but think about how it was so much like Zane—on its own, standing apart, quietly magnificent.

He opened one of three garage bays and pulled the car inside. Two other gleaming sports cars and a motorcycle were already parked there. Zane had done well for himself with his business. That much was clear. He turned off the ignition, and they were both noticeably rushing to get inside. He opened the door for her, shut off his security system via a keypad and took her hand, marching through the mostly dark house. They traveled through an unbelievable kitchen, nearly three times the size of Allison's back in LA, then down a central hall toward the back of the house. Allison was busy trying to look at everything—she wanted to soak up every bit of Zane's tastes. She wanted to scrutinize the artwork and try to speculate about what had drawn him to the pieces he'd chosen. She wanted to do the same with furniture and paint colors. She wanted to know him inside and out.

"A tour would be nice," she said when they'd reached a set of tall double doors at the end of the hall.

Zane pushed them open and flipped a light switch. "I know. Let's start here."

Allison stepped into the most stunning, jaw-dropping bedroom she'd ever seen, which was saying a lot since Zane was adjusting the dimmer to a level fit for seduction. The space was like something out of a magazine, with a soaring cathedral ceiling, a spacious seating area to one side with a modern charcoal-gray sectional sofa and a TV, and at the very center of the room, a gorgeously appointed bed. She took her chance to run her hand over the crisp white duvet, the threads silky beneath her touch. This room was nothing short of sheer perfection.

Zane came up behind her, gripping her shoulders and pressing his long frame against her back. He kissed her neck softly, bringing her body to a gentle boil. "Do you approve?"

Allison's eyes drifted shut, luxuriating in the action of his lips as he skimmed them over the delicate spot beneath her ear. "Which part? The room or your amazing mouth?"

He spun her around and wrapped her up in his arms, drawing her flat against his chest and kissing her deeply. His tongue wasn't playing—he was determined, consumed by a drive she could not see, but could certainly feel. "You were all I could think about last night. And this morning. And all day at work."

"Really?" she asked, grinning to herself in the dark.

"Yes, really."

"What were you thinking?" She'd shared her fantasy with him...if he'd taken the time to think up one about her, she wanted to hear it. Every last word.

"About you and the sarong." He dug his fingers into her hair, gently tugging at her nape to encourage her to drop her head to one side.

"I'm listening. What else?"

His mouth, hot and wet, skated down the length of her neck, settling in the slope where it met her shoulder. One hand went to the zipper on her dress, slowly drawing it down while the other grabbed her backside. "I'm not as good at this as you are."

"Something tells me you could be great at this if you just applied yourself." She untucked his shirt and threaded her hands underneath it, exploring the landscape of his muscled back. "Don't think too much about it. Just tell me what happens with me and you and the sarong." To encourage him, she placed one hand flat on his crotch and rubbed his erection through his dress pants.

A raspy groan escaped his throat. "I untie it. I take it off."

She unhooked his belt, unbuttoned his trousers and unzipped them. Slipping her hand down the front of his boxer briefs, she caressed his solid length with her fingers. "Good. What else?"

"In my fantasy, you're already naked. No bathing suit." With a pop, he undid the clasp of her bra, then pulled the dress and the rest of the ensemble forward, leaving her chest bare to him. "I love your breasts. They're so perfect. Silky and velvety. I love the way they fit in my hands. So I do this." He lowered his head, cupped both breasts with his hands and swirled his tongue around her nipple. Teasing. Flicking. Then sucking.

Allison's eyes fluttered shut as white flames of lust seemed to envelop her thighs. She was so hot for him already. Having him tell her what he liked about her body was only heightening the experience. "That feels so good, Zane. You have no idea."

He dropped to his knees, pulling her dress down to the floor. She kicked her heels off, and he sat back on his haunches, gazing up at her like she was a goddess. "You didn't have these panties on in my fantasy, but I like them. They're sexy." He hooked his finger under the waistband of her lacy black undies, traveling from one hip to the other, just gently grazing her most delicate area at the center. "But they need to go." He tugged them past her hips, leaving her to step out of them. Then he stood back up. "In my fantasy, you're so wet for me."

Allison thought she might melt into a puddle. She also knew she couldn't take so little nakedness from him. Her fingers flew through the buttons of his shirt as he reached down between her legs, separating her delicate folds with his fingers.

"Yes. Exactly like this." He rubbed her apex firmly in a circle, kissing her neck again, using his tongue to drive her wild. With every rotation of his hand, he was sending her toward her peak. Pushing her closer to the edge.

"I want you. There's no hiding it." It took every ounce of strength she had to push his pants to the floor, but she had to have him in her hand. She needed to even the score between them. She stroked firmly, from base to tip, and kissed his chest. "What comes next?"

"Then I make love to you in several gravity-defying positions." He laughed against his lips. "I turned myself into quite the performer in this fantasy."

She smiled, but she wanted to explore this idea. She wanted to know his steamiest thoughts and act on them. "Show me."

"Really?" He ran his tongue along his lower lip, showing her his trepidation.

"Yes." She nodded and looked him right in the eye, wanting him to know how serious she was.

"Okay, then." He took her hand and led her over to the bedside table, where he opened a drawer and pulled out a box of condoms. He handed her the foil packet. "In my fantasy, you put it on for me."

"Accuracy is very important in a fantasy." She took her time, tearing it open, then carefully rolling it on, eliciting a groan of pleasure from Zane as she did it.

"Up against the wall." She stepped to the side of the table, where there was an expanse of open space. She placed her back to the wall, and he reached down for one of her legs and hitched it over his hip.

Allison wrapped her calf around him and watched as he took his erection in his hand and positioned himself at her entrance. He drove about halfway inside, taking her breath away, then pulled her other leg up around him. Her body weight rested against the wall, but his hands cradled her backside. This angle was incredibly gratifying from the start—it let her sink deep down onto him, centering the pressure in the ideal spot. She rocked her hips forward and back, her entire body buzzing with pleasure. She was close. So close.

"Was it like this?" She dug her fingers into his hair and kissed him, relishing the tension in his body right now—the flex of his biceps and forearms as he held her up and the tautness of his abs with every stroke.

"This is better," he said. "You're better in real life. The stuff that's in my head doesn't come close to the real you." The kiss he laid on her then was one for the ages, intense and raw. Honest and sincere. It sent her body over the edge, the peak rattling her to her very core, shaking her physically and mentally. Zane followed right after, pressing her harder against the wall as he rode out the waves of pleasure.

For a moment, neither said a thing, breaths coming fast and heavy as they coiled themselves around each other tighter. A thought flashed in her head, and she dared to utter it. "The fantasy just isn't enough anymore, Zane. I need this. So much more of this."

Zane's mind and body were reeling in the best possible way. It took every ounce of energy he had left to carry her over to the bed and set her down without dropping her. He was wonderfully spent.

He tossed aside the throw pillows littering the bed, then pulled back the duvet. Both a bit delirious, they found their way under the covers, immediately drawn to each other. Allison curled into his body and kissed his chest. He loved having her in his bed. As amazing as things had been on the island, this was different. The fantasy world had fallen away, but even framed by his everyday reality, being with Allison felt like a dream. Was he falling for her? The perpetual bachelor? His mom had certainly made a compelling case for his finally jettisoning those ways.

"You're so amazing," she muttered.

"You're the amazing one." The words came so fast. He didn't even have to think about them. That was it—he really had fallen. He'd gone through life telling himself that he wouldn't let it happen. He'd seen what it did to his parents when love fell apart. There was no way that risking that much pain could ever be worth it. But being here with Allison and knowing that his heart wanted nothing else made him realize that there was no way to build up an immunity to love. It had taken the right woman to show him that. The perfect woman. Allison. He caressed her naked back with his hand. "No argument?" He'd half expected her to dispute his claim that she was the amazing one. Instead, she was being incredibly still and quiet. He must have really sent her to the moon and back. She'd certainly done that for him.

"I'm thinking."

"About what?"

"Everything."

He smiled in the dark. "Me, too." So many thoughts were swirling around in his head, all of them surprisingly good. When had things ever been like that? No time in recent history, that was for sure.

"I need to tell you something."

He'd been about to say the exact same thing, but she'd gotten to it first. "What is it?"

She drew in a breath so deep her entire body rose and fell in the cradle of his arm. "What I'm about to say… I just… I don't want you to get upset. But I would understand if you did." She rolled away from him and switched on the lamp on her side of the bed.

He squinted at the bright light. It got Zane's attention, and not just because he was enjoying the view of her naked backside while she was turned away. He sat up in bed. "Okay." Whatever she was about to say, he wanted to just get past it. He was tired of bad news and dire circumstances keeping him from happiness. Whatever it was, they would find a way around it. "Please. Just tell me. I can take it."

She grabbed a corner of the comforter and covered herself up. "First off, the job I'm working on here in Falling Brook is going really well. They've put me on retainer for the next month, and if things go the way I think they will, it will become permanent. They would be a big enough client for me to move back to Falling Brook. To stay here in town."

The relief Zane felt was immense. It was like someone had been standing on his chest and they'd finally stepped off. "That's amazing. I'm so happy for you." In truth, he was happy for *them*. Long distance would have been terrible and certainly no way for them to truly move forward together. Now he had one less thing to worry about.

"Thanks. I'm really happy about it, too. I've worked really hard for this."

Now that he'd had a minute for this news to sink in, his brain was starting to catch up. Falling Brook was a small town. Most businesspeople who lived here were CEOs or senior management for big corporations in the city, not local operations like Zane's. But who could it be? "And this company is based right here in town?"

"Yes, but hold on a minute. Before I get to that, I need to tell you that I realized tonight that I can't make the decision to stay here in Falling Brook until we have a discussion about us. And I don't want to hit you with some big heavy talk right now, especially after we just had totally mind-blowing sex, but I can't move back here and see you on the street or at the Java Hut and not be able to walk up to you and hug you. Kiss you and hold your hand. I've done that before and it nearly killed me."

Now he was starting to see where she was coming from, and he was totally on board. In fact, he couldn't ignore the happy feeling in his heart. She wanted him and he wanted her, for more than just sex. "So we need to come clean with Scott. I completely agree. We can either do it together or if you want, I can tell him on my own and then you guys can have your own talk. But no matter what, I think we need to make it clear that this isn't us asking him for permission. In the end, we're our own people.

We make our own decisions. We have to do what's right for us."

She dropped her shoulders, seeming frustrated. "Yes. I completely agree. That is all true and that does need to happen. Right away. But first, there's one more thing I have to tell you."

An unsettling quiet filled the room. "Is this the thing that might upset me?"

"Yes."

His heart hammered. "Please tell me. Say it and get it over with."

"The client is Black Crescent."

The blood drained from Zane's face so fast that it made him sick. This couldn't possibly be happening. No. Absolutely not. How could what was starting to work out perfectly take such a nightmarish turn? "You're working for Black Crescent." He sat up a little straighter in bed. "You, quite possibly the most decent and upstanding person I know, are working for the most evil and vile company imaginable. You're working for the devil. Why would you do that?" With every word out of his mouth, his disgust grew. "Why would you even entertain the idea?"

"Zane, come on. Isn't that all a little overdramatic?"

Zane had been trying to keep himself in check, but that word pissed him off. He'd had it lobbed at him before, and he disliked it greatly. He threw back the covers and scrambled out of bed, plucking his underwear from the floor and putting them back on. He was so full of anger right now it felt like it might bubble up out the top of his head. He had to move to keep his mind straight. And he couldn't be naked in bed with Allison anymore. "Is that why you said all of that stuff to me on the island about letting it go? Is that why you were being so secretive about your work calls?" He ran his hand through his hair, pacing back and forth across his bedroom floor. "Does that Ryan guy work for BC? No wonder I had a bad feeling about him."

"Ryan is a candidate to take Joshua Lowell's place."

Zane's stomach turned. "So the guy you were talking to while we were on the island is going to be the new Josh Lowell? That's just awesome." He sincerely hoped the sarcasm was hitting home for her. He didn't want to be a jerk again, but he needed her to understand how hurt he was right now.

"Maybe. He's just interviewing right now. Actually, you should meet him. He's a really nice guy. I think you would like him. I think you would like all of the people who are interviewing for the job."

Zane made a point of looking at her as though she'd lost her mind. He didn't want to ask the question out loud, but he wasn't afraid to suggest it by other means. This entire line of thinking was so off base.

"Honestly," she continued. "I think you would really like Josh if you got to know him. In a lot of ways, he's just as much a victim of his dad as you are. None of what happened was your fault, but it wasn't his fault, either."

And to think, Zane had been so sure that Allison understood him. Now he knew that he was wrong. So very wrong. "That's okay. I think I'll skip the part of this scenario where you whip up some dream of Josh Lowell and me becoming best friends. I realize that it's your special talent to come up with fantasies."

"That's really mean. And completely uncalled for."

"It's the truth."

Allison grumbled under her breath. "You know what, Zane? Screw you. That's not what I was suggesting. All I'm saying is that I think you need to take a deep breath, try to take a step back and look at this from my perspective. You can't undo what happened, okay? You need to let it go. I'm sorry, but you do. At some point, you're going to have to get over this or you're just going to be stuck forever."

Zane disliked a lot of things, but he despised it when anyone told him to get over Black Crescent. His entire life had been ground into the dirt by the greed of the Lowell family. He and his parents had been treated like they were nothing, taken for their family fortune and cast aside, with absolutely zero repercussions for those who committed the crime. That injustice sat in the depths of his belly every day. He couldn't "just get over it." It was impossible. "I'm not talking about this anymore. You were there for the fallout. You know how badly I was hurt. You saw it firsthand. I not only shouldn't have to explain it to you, I won't."

"I'm sure you're going to say this is just a cliché, but every black cloud has a silver lining. If Vernon Lowell hadn't taken off with that money, you and I never would have met. You and Scott wouldn't have the friendship you have today. Black Crescent isn't all bad. I wish that you could see that."

"And I wish you could see why that is beside the point." He scanned her face, desperate for some sign of the Allison he so adored. Right now, it was hard to imagine he'd dared to think about the future with her. How could he have been so stupid? "I think you should go home."

"Seriously?"

"Seriously."

Allison whipped back the comforter and grabbed her dress from the floor where it had landed earlier. She threaded her arms through it, wrapped it around her body and zipped it. "You drove me here. I'm not using a ride app this time of night. I've heard too many scary stories about women ending up with creepy drivers."

Zane plucked his pants from the floor and fished his car keys out of the pocket. "Take my car. I'll get it back from you later." He tossed them to her.

She caught them, staring down at her hand for a moment. "Oh, right. Zane Patterson, the golden boy, the super successful entrepreneur, has an entire garage full of cars. He has them to spare."

"That's right. That's me. Mr. Perfect." Right now, he felt as far from that as he'd quite possibly ever felt. If that was what Allison truly thought, she'd lost it. So had his mom, for that matter.

"Goodbye, Zane. I'll let myself out." She pivoted on her heel and headed for the bedroom door.

"You *knew* this was going to happen, Allison. You knew this would be my reaction. Nothing about the conversation we just had should come as any surprise. And you knew it the whole time we were on the island, didn't you?"

She stopped in the doorway and turned back to him. "I'd foolishly hoped for a better outcome."

"You don't understand what this is like for me."

She shook her head with a pitying look in her eyes. "I do understand it, Zane. And I don't know what I have to do to convince you of that."

Twelve

Scott bellowed at the guest room door. "Zane Patterson, I know you're in there. Get out here. You have some explaining to do."

Allison pried open one eye and looked at the alarm clock on the bedside table. The numbers were a bit blurry, probably because she'd taken a sleeping pill last night after her big knock-down, drag-out fight with Zane. She was only half-awake.

Boom boom boom. Scott pounded on the door. "Up and at 'em, you two."

Allison scrambled out of bed. She wanted to shut her brother up before he woke up the entire house. She did *not* want her niece and nephew thinking the worst of her. She opened the door, leaving a space just wide enough to talk to him. "He's not here. Will you please be quiet? It's freaking six thirty in the morning."

"You know I get up early to work out."

"Good for you. I'm going back to bed." She left the door ajar and shuffled across the room, flopping down on the mattress. Her motivation was gone. In a lot of ways, it felt like her whole life was gone. She didn't want to work today. She didn't want to talk to anyone or go anywhere. She wanted to call in sick to life.

Unfortunately, Scott had followed her into the room and was standing at the foot of the bed. "Why is his car outside?"

"He gave it to me to drive home last night. He has several cars, you know. He gave me an extra." Last night was still a blur. It had started so amazingly and gone so incredibly wrong. She'd worried that Zane would take the Black Crescent news badly, but she'd underestimated the scope. She'd certainly never imagined he'd toss her out of his house.

"What in the world is going on, Alli?"

Allison sat up in bed and scooted back until she was leaning against the headboard. She blew out a breath of frustration and crossed her arms over her chest. Was she really ready to spill the beans to Scott? This was not going to be a fun conversation. But she had to take what had been handed to her, fun or not. She patted the mattress. "Come. Sit."

Scott joined her, but she sensed that he was deeply uncomfortable. He was sitting like he had a board strapped to his back. His shoulders were tight, as was his whole face. He had to know what was coming next.

"Zane and I slept together when we were in the Bahamas."

"I knew it." He practically pounced on her with his words. "I knew that was going to happen. I warned you, and you just couldn't listen to me, could you? I'm just the lame older brother who's too heavy-handed with advice."

"I didn't listen because I didn't want to, okay? Scott, you need to know that I have had a thing for Zane since I was a teenager. We're talking fifteen years. I always hoped that it would go away, but it just didn't."

"What? No way. I would've seen it."

She pressed her lips together tightly. The years of longing for Zane would always bring a sting to her eyes, but they especially did now. "I'm serious. I'm just really good at hiding it. I can always put on a good face."

"So when you guys were acting so odd at my party, was that part of it?"

"We kissed that night."

"Ugh." His voice was rife with disgust. "Did you guys make a plan to meet up at Rose Cove? Has this been in the works the whole time?"

She shook her head. "No. It was just dumb luck, believe it or not." Now it felt like tragic luck. If it hadn't happened, her heart wouldn't be in tatters.

Scott got up from the bed and began pacing. "I love him, but I'm going to kill him. I told him you were off-limits, and he completely disrespected my wishes."

She pinched the bridge of her nose and made an inward plea for strength. "Will you stop jumping to conclusions and let me talk, please?"

He turned back to her with a distinct scowl on his face. "So talk."

"When I kissed him, he freaked out. He said he could never betray you. That's why he left that night. And it was a big topic of conversation on the island. He refused to let it go. Believe me, Zane put your wishes first."

"Until he didn't."

"Until *we* didn't. It was both of us. We both wanted to do it, and we both knew exactly what we were doing."

Scott grimaced. "Please. Spare me the details."

Allison rolled her eyes. "I'm only saying that it was two adults doing what adults do. We were in a very intense situation with the storm and I guess that just made everything that much more heightened. As soon as we were rescued, he wanted things to go back to the way they were before."

"Really?"

"Really."

"So then what happened last night?"

She shrugged. "He had second thoughts, I guess. So we went back to his place."

Scott held up a hand to keep her from saying more. "Okay. I got it. But I don't understand. He made you drive yourself home?"

She shook her head. "Unfortunately, I had to tell him about Black Crescent. Things went really well there yesterday and I don't think it's going to be a onetime job. Joshua Lowell is putting in a good word for me, and he's put me on retainer for the next month. I was going to tell you yesterday, but I never had the chance."

Scott drew in a deep breath through his nose, the gears in his head clearly turning. "What did Zane say? Did he hit the roof?"

"He did. But then it snowballed from there and he just sort of shut down. That's when he asked me to leave. That's why I have his car."

"So what now? Is it over?"

Allison froze as a single tear rolled down her cheek. As upset as she'd been last night, she hadn't cried. But something about those three words—*is it over?*—made the dam break. "I don't know. I don't want to think that last night was the end, but I just don't know. He has such a grudge when it comes to Black Crescent and the Lowells. It's so frustrating."

"Well, of course it is, but it's not like there isn't

a good reason for it. The scars you get as a young person are always the ones that feel the deepest. It's just the way life is."

Allison had never thought of it that way. She'd never seen a parallel between her life and Zane's. Until now. Her brother was right. The pain she had from years of Zane being her unrequited love was very real. And there was something about it that had always felt especially raw. She hadn't been able to start exploring it until the kiss at Scott's party, but it hit her hardest at Rose Cove. A single "no" from Zane was far more devastating than any rejection she'd ever experienced. "Yeah. I suppose you're right."

"And as the person with a front-row seat when his family fell apart, I can tell you that it was incredibly difficult for him. The number of nights we sat up with him talking and me listening? I couldn't begin to count. I don't really know that I was equipped to help him through it. All I could do was listen and be his friend. I'm guessing the guy needs some therapy."

"You're probably right, but that doesn't help at the moment. I don't know what to do to make any of this better, and I hate feeling so helpless. I feel like screaming. Isn't love more important than any of this? Isn't it supposed to conquer all?"

Now it was Scott's turn to remain perfectly still. "Do you love him?"

She nodded, her sadness morphing into conviction to put it all out there with her brother. She had to make this declaration to somebody, even if nothing ever came of it. "I do. The big dumb jerk. I love him. And I don't know what to say or do to help him get past this."

Scott sat back down on the bed and took her hands. "This is why I didn't want you to get involved with him. I never want to see you get hurt."

Allison saw her chance to finally sort this out with brother, hopefully once and for all. "Scott, life hurts. Love hurts. I don't want to sit on the sidelines and be an observer. I can take care of myself, and if I get hurt, I'll be okay. Even now, with my heart in twenty pieces, I know that I'll be okay. I have a good career and great friends and an amazing family I love more than anything. I know you still look at me and see that sick little girl in the hospital bed, but that isn't me anymore, and it hasn't been me for a long time."

Scott's eyes misted. He was a tough-as-nails guy, but this got to him. "I realize that I was just a kid when it happened, but I've never been as scared as I was when you were sick. Never."

Allison felt like her heart was going to break every time she listened to Scott or one of her parents talk about this. She hated that it was still so raw for them, but they'd all understood that it was a matter of life and death. She'd been too young to understand, but she wanted to believe that she did now. "I know, honey. But I'm fine. I'm here. And you need to let it go."

He cleared his throat and collected himself. "Just like Zane needs to let Black Crescent go?"

Apparently they all had things they needed to let go of. "Yes. If you can figure out how to make him do that, I'd love to hear your suggestions." From the bedside table, her phone beeped with a text. Her brain flew to the thought that it might be Zane, but when she consulted the screen, her heart sank with disappointment. It wasn't him. "Speak of the devil. It's Joshua Lowell. He wants me to come in to the BC offices this morning."

"A little early for a work text, isn't it?"

"Apparently he's like you. He doesn't like to sleep in, either."

Zane hadn't slept at all. Not a damn minute. And he couldn't begin to process what he was feeling. Every time he followed one line of thought, he got distracted by another. He'd start to think about Black Crescent, familiar anger and pain welling up inside him. The fact that his feelings about BC were now tied to Allison made it even more difficult to sort any of it out. Her betrayal ran deep, registering in the center of his chest and causing him physical pain. Allison knew how he felt about Black Crescent. She'd not only witnessed the initial fallout all those years ago, he'd told her everything he was still feeling when they were in the Bahamas. And she hadn't said a thing. Not a peep. That hurt most of all. They'd made love, and she'd known that what she was doing would hurt him. She'd known it all along.

There was no telling how any of this would work out. When he tried to see his future—the days and weeks beyond now—he still saw Allison there. He'd seen her there last night before everything fell apart, and now in the light of day, she was still there. He didn't want to imagine tomorrow, the next day or the day after that without her. She'd opened something up in him on the island. She'd done it again last night. It didn't feel as though he could shut the door on that, even if he wanted to. So how was he going to get past this?

One thing Allison had said last night kept bubbling to the surface—how every black cloud had a silver lining. How BC had ruined one thing, but it had brought them together. It wasn't all bad, as much as he'd always seen it as such. And Allison in particular was easily the best thing that had happened to him ever. He couldn't fathom walking away from that. From her. It made no sense.

The realization made his end of the conversation from last night sting. He'd said some horrible things. He'd stupidly let his anger take control, as was so often the case with BC. If he was ever going to move forward in his life, he had to force himself to stop allowing what had happened with BC to define him.

He was stronger than that. He knew that. He'd simply let his anger get the best of him.

He had to talk this out with Allison. He had to explain himself to Scott. He had to open himself up to the fact that he'd been wrong about more than a few things. His own mother had proved him wrong yesterday. Allison had done the same with everything she'd said about silver linings. And now he had to talk to her. To find a way through the mess he'd created from years of clinging to anger and resentment. This was about more than making amends. This was about making a future. He had to find Allison. Luckily, he knew exactly where to look.

He jumped in the shower, hoping a little hot water and soap might help to reset his head. He couldn't begin to figure out where to start with Allison. There was a part of him that wanted to confess his feelings and hope that would be enough to make her step away from Black Crescent. There was another part of him that wanted an apology. There was yet another piece of his soul that knew he should be the one to say he was sorry. He hated that his feelings were so jumbled out of control. He hated that he couldn't let everything go after all these years.

Freshly shaven and dressed for work, he drove his Porsche over to Scott's house. When he arrived, his BMW was parked out front, but Allison's zippy silver rental was noticeably absent from the driveway. Hopefully Scott had let her put it in the garage.

He wasn't worried that she'd left town. Black Crescent was keeping her here for the foreseeable future. But he was concerned that she might not be home. He wasn't eager to chase her all over Falling Brook, but he would if that was his only option. He had to sort this out, and the only logical path started and ended with Allison.

He rang the doorbell, then stuffed his hands in his pockets. He'd never before been nervous to arrive at his best friend's house, and the feeling was unsettling.

Scott flung the door open, sweating profusely and wiping it from his forehead with a towel. "Looking for your car keys, I take it?" Scott's voice had a cutting edge. His best friend had never before taken that tone with him. He disliked it greatly.

"I'm actually looking for Allison. Is she here?" Zane peered around his best friend. "Can I come in?"

"I don't know, Zane. Right now, I'm trying to keep from punching you in the face."

At least Zane now knew that the cat was out of the bag. Clearly, Scott had been briefed on the state of his relationship with Allison. "You know I'll hit you right back, and then where will we be? Fighting in the middle of your front lawn for all of your fine and upstanding neighbors to see."

Scott stepped back and opened the front door wider. "Fine. Come in." He closed it as soon as Zane walked past him. "I could literally kill you for sleeping with Allison. How could you treat her like one of your hookups? She's my damn sister. You're my best friend, for God's sake."

Zane turned back to Scott. The guilt he bore from his own actions was eclipsed by his best friend's misguided characterization of what had happened. "I did *not* treat her like a hookup. I care about her. Deeply." He felt the wobble in his own voice before he heard it. As if he needed any more confirmation that he was in deep with Allison. "That's why I'm here. I need to talk to her."

"She left about ten minutes ago."

"It's not even eight o'clock. Where did she go?"

"I'm not sure I should tell you."

Zane swallowed the bile that rose in his throat. His best friend still felt the need to protect his sister from Zane. He had to put an end to that. "Look, man, you and I have got to get past this. I know I crossed a line, but you need to know that I did not do it without thinking about it hard, and for a very long time. I fought our attraction as long as I could, but in the end, Allison made a compelling case. I'm drawn to her, and she's drawn to me. We work well together, and we care a lot about each other." Zane directed his gaze down at his feet, knowing he wasn't 100 percent certain about her side of that assertion. "Well, I care deeply about her. I think she cares about me."

"Yeah?" Scott asked, seeming unimpressed.

"Yes, Scott. I care about her. I want to see where that can go."

"You. The guy with the revolving door in his pants."

"Hey. Am I not entitled to want more? Do I not get to change the direction of my life because I've found the right girl and I want to be with her? You found that with Brittney, and you're happy. In fact, you love to remind me of it. All the time." Zane again looked Scott square in the eye. "Please don't torpedo our friendship because I'm looking for the same thing that you have. It's not fair."

Scott drew a deep breath through his nose and leaned against the doorway into the dining room. "You have to swear to me that you will not intentionally hurt her."

"Of course."

"You promise?"

"Yes."

Scott clapped his hand on Zane's shoulder. "Okay then. You have my blessing."

"Now tell me where she is."

"She's at Black Crescent."

Just when Zane thought he couldn't take another shock to the system, he got another. Black Crescent was the exact last place on the planet he wanted to visit. Was this the universe's way of forcing him to deal with every sticking point in his life all on one day? If that was the case, bring it on. He was done letting BC define him. He certainly wasn't going to let it stand in the way of what he really wanted—Allison. "Got it. Thanks." Zane reached for the doorknob.

"Don't make a fool of yourself, okay?"

Zane opened the door. "I won't embarrass Allison, if that's what you're trying to say. I would never put her job in jeopardy."

"Good."

"As for me, I've already made myself look like an idiot. Things can't get any worse." With that, Zane rushed down the driveway to his car. He knew that his conversation with Scott was as close as they would ever come to working things out in regard to Allison. If this next part went well, he and Scott would hopefully return to their affable, hyper-competitive dynamic. Another outcome to wish for.

"I can't believe I'm doing this," he muttered to himself when he pulled into the Black Crescent parking lot. He'd come here a few short weeks ago to come clean to Joshua Lowell about the anonymous DNA report he'd received and shared. Unfortunately, Josh had left the office. It took several hours, but Zane had been able to track him down in a bar in the neighboring town. Zane wished he could erase that entire chapter of his personal story with BC. He never should have gotten involved. He never should have let Josh get under his skin.

He pulled into a space with a decent view of the entrance, rolled down the windows and sent a text to his assistant letting her know that at best, he'd be late getting in the office. In truth, he hoped against hope that he and Allison could work everything out and he wouldn't feel driven to go to work at all.

An hour passed. Then another. He knew better than to waltz into that office and ask for her, but damn he was tempted. He didn't want to wait. Impatience was gnawing at him. But he stayed put, running through the words he wanted to say, praying that somehow it all worked out. Even with all that preparation, he wasn't truly ready when Allison walked out of the BC building, looking like a million bucks in a sleek black skirt, white blouse and heels. She was smiling. A big, wide grin. And it stole more than a breath. It knocked the wind out of him.

The Zane of old would've allowed her facial expression to send him into a downward spiral. How could anyone walk out of that building and be happy? But he knew that his old thinking had gotten him nowhere. It had left him running in circles. Allison's business was important to her. It must have been a good meeting. He had to believe that whatever had happened in that building had made her happy. And that made *him* happy, which was yet another reason to see BC in a different light. Yes, his old life had been ended by forces within that company. But his new life, the one that left him with a sliver of a chance with Allison Randall, had started at the same time.

He jumped out of his car and called her name. "Allison!"

She startled, then swiped off her sunglasses. "Zane? You came to Black Crescent? Are you insane?"

"Maybe a little," he muttered to himself.

"What in the world are you doing here?" she asked, incredulous, marching toward him.

He rushed over to her and didn't wait another minute to just come out with it. "I'm sorry. So sorry about last night. I was wrong."

She shook her head. "No, Zane. I was wrong. I should've told you back on the island. Before anything happened. That was wrong of me, and I'm sorry that I did it."

Relief washed over him in a deluge. All was not lost. He took her hand, loving the feel of her silky skin against his. "It's okay. I forgive you."

"If anything, it should tell you how much I was worried about messing things up with you. I had to have my chance, and I couldn't bring myself to jeopardize it by coming clean."

He brought her hand to his lips and kissed it. He wanted to be able to do that every day. Forever and ever. "That's the sweetest thing anyone has ever said to me."

She turned for an instant and glanced back at the building. "I hope you know it's just a job. I mean, I will kick some serious butt for them, but it's what I do. It's not out of some grand allegiance to the company or the Lowell family. It's out of a commitment to being a professional, working hard and supporting myself and Kianna. That's all it is."

He nodded. "I know. And I get it. You weren't afraid to do the thing no one would've expected you to do. You're great at taking chances. It's something I need to get better at."

"I took a chance when I kissed you that first time."

"That's the perfect example. I need to stop playing it safe." He swallowed back the emotion of the moment, of how much she meant to him and how grateful he was that she'd stuck around and kept pushing when he'd been doing nothing but putting up walls. He was so lucky to have her in his life. "When you've lost everything, it's just easier to play it safe. Don't risk a thing. Don't put anything of importance on the line. Friendship. Your heart. But then you came along and took my heart from me. You have it, Alli."

She cocked her head to one side. "I do?"

"Yes. And I don't want it back." He took her hand and pressed it flat against the center of his chest. It had hurt so badly that morning, and now it was nothing but impossibly warm. A single touch from her and he was healed. "I want you to keep it forever. Promise me that you'll hold on to it. I love you, Allison Randall, and I don't want you to ever forget that."

Her eyes lit up, bright and brilliant. "Oh, God, Zane. I love you, too." She gripped his elbows and leaned into him. "I think I've loved you since the moment I met you."

His heart felt as though it had swelled to twice its normal size. He hadn't realized how little hope he had that she'd return the sentiment until the words crossed her lovely lips. They fell into the most memorable kiss yet—it was an unspoken promise, wrapped up in years of friendship, tied with a wish for forever.

They came up for air, and he rested his forehead against hers, holding her close, not wanting to let her go ever. "I want it all with you, Allison. I realize it hasn't even been a week since we first slept together, but I know that the foundation is there between us. I don't want to wait to build our life together. The two of us. Forever and ever. Husband and wife. Best friends. Platinum bands and wedding bells."

She bit down on her lower lip. "A Rose Cove honeymoon in a cottage up on the hill?"

"Will it make you say yes?"

"I don't need a trip to an island to know that I'll love you forever, Zane. Of course I'm saying yes. A million times yes."

Epilogue

One month later

Angelique and Allison's mom walked into Angelique's bedroom at the exact right moment—Kianna was putting the finishing touches on Allison's bridal hair.

"So beautiful," her mom said, smiling, then kissing Allison on the cheek.

"The most beautiful," Angelique added.

Allison's heart was already so full of love, she wasn't sure how she'd survive the wedding. She knew she'd better prepare. There was only a half hour until they'd walk from Angelique and Hubert's house for the dock at Rose Cove. From there, Marcus would be taking everyone via boat to Mako Island. Zane had decided it was only fitting that they get married there. He liked the idea that no one else would ever be able to say that their wedding had taken place on that particular patch of sand in the Caribbean.

As for Allison, she was simply glad that they'd decided to have the ceremony be a small and informal affair. Only so many people could fit on Mako Island, so they'd kept the guest list small—Scott, Brittney and the kids, Zane's mom and dad, Allison's parents, Angelique and Hubert, and Kianna. The dress code was decidedly casual—bare feet and flip-flops, shorts and sundresses, hats and sunglasses. Allison had gone with a new white bathing suit—a simple one-piece for modesty since her parents were in attendance, but with a plunging back for Zane's required sexy factor. A white sarong embroidered with silver threads wrapped at her waist completed the look. Zane had once said that he loved her flair for fashion, and she was happy her bridal ensemble perfectly reflected her individual style. She could not have gotten away with this getup in Falling Brook. All the more reason to be glad to be far away from that.

"It's so amazing that you were able to get the guest cottages fixed up in time for the wedding," Kianna said to Angelique. "From everything Allison said, things were pretty messy."

"My husband was highly motivated. He had a crew out here as soon as Alli called to tell us the news. He didn't want her second visit this year to Rose Cove to be anything less than perfect," Angelique said. "It was mostly water damage. Luckily, all of the building structures rode out the storm just fine."

"I'm so glad," Allison said. "It could've been so much worse." Although that scary weather event had caused so much heartache, she was still oddly thankful for it. It forced her and Zane to get past their other issues. It brought them together. If it hadn't happened, she might have spent the rest of her vacation holed up in her cottage, mad at Zane. And the rest of her life feeling as though something big was missing.

"How is your husband doing?" Kianna asked Angelique.

"Hubert is a new man. The doctor gave him a clean bill of health, so it looks like we're in the clear, which is a huge relief."

A knock came at the door and Brittney poked her head inside. "I think they're ready for you. It's only forty-five minutes until sunset."

"Angelique, we'd better get the flowers," Allison's mom said. "We'll meet you on the boat, sweetheart." She cupped Allison's face. "I love you. Always."

Moments like that reminded Allison how precious her family's love was. It wasn't a burden as she'd sometimes felt. "I love you, too, Mom."

Angelique and her mom left, while Kianna made one final adjustment to the tropical flowers in Allison's hair.

"Thank you for being here for this," Allison said. "I know it's a pain to fly across the country to spend time in Falling Brook, then all the way down here."

She shook her head. "Do not thank me. I'm over the moon to be here. I couldn't feel more honored. Plus, I'd better get used to flying great distances to see you."

"You're sure you're okay with us running a bi-coastal operation?"

"I don't want to do it forever, if that's what you're asking, but I'm cool with it for the next several years. You got a one-month extension on the Black Crescent retainer, and we'll see how that plays out. Sounds like your future hubby wants us to do some recruiting for his company, and I figure it's just another selling point for potential clients that we can say we have offices in New Jersey and LA."

"Yes. I think so, too. We can cover the entire country. No problem."

"I will say, however, that if you decide to find a wealthy CEO in Falling Brook to set me up with, I could be very happy becoming an East Coast company, too."

"Really? You liked Falling Brook?"

Kianna shrugged. "I did. I can also admit to being a bit jealous. You have it all, girl. A beautiful place to live and the best man ever. Zane is a dream come true. If I can find a guy half that good, I'll be happy."

"You'll find him." She thought about it for a minute. "Although if it might get you to move to New Jersey, I might have to start looking for him myself. In earnest."

"Executive recruiter and matchmaker. I like it." Kianna unleashed her megawatt smile, her cheeks plumping up. "That could end up being your ultimate calling."

"I'm on it. As soon as I get married."

They walked down the crushed-shell path toward the dock, where the rest of the guests would be waiting on the boat. Zane and Scott had gone out to Mako Island an hour earlier so they could spend some time talking and Allison could still make her traditional bride's entrance. Scott and Zane's friendship had not only withstood the test of the romance between Allison and Zane, it had come out on the other side much stronger. Both Zane and Scott had admitted as much to Allison—not voluntarily; she'd had to drag it out of each of them separately. She was glad they had each other. She was relieved that hadn't gone away.

When Allison and Kianna approached the boat, the gathered family all stood and clapped. Allison felt a rush of pleasant warmth to her face. She didn't relish being the center of attention, but on this day, she lapped it up. They were soon on their way, the warm sea breezes brushing against her skin while the sky turned the most brilliant shades of pink and orange as the sun began to make its descent. Her heart picked up in anticipation when she caught sight of tiny Mako Island and could see those two tall figures standing on the beach—Scott and Zane. Her two favorite guys.

Marcus carefully motored the boat into the shallowest navigable water, then set anchor, instructed Allison's dad to roll up his pant legs and helped to guide everyone through the knee-high depths to shore. They all gathered under the shade of the largest palm with Scott standing at the center. He'd been ordained via the internet for the occasion, and was quite proud of his job as officiant, although Zane and Allison had designed the ceremony to be ultra-short and sweet. Zane was to his left, and even from this far away, with Allison still standing on the boat in the bobbing water, she could see how happy and relaxed he was. She hoped he could spend as many days of his life as possible looking and feeling that way. He deserved it. They both did.

Finally, it was Allison's turn to be helped off the boat. Her dad was standing only a few feet away, ready to walk her down the aisle, or, more specifically, across the sandy bottom. She kissed his cheek, then hooked her arm in his and snugged him closer.

"I love you, Alli," he said as they began their father-daughter ocean stroll.

"I love you, too, Dad. So much."

Ahead, all Allison could see was Zane, the man of her dreams. His heartbreaking smile seemed like a permanent fixture on his handsome face, which was exactly the way she liked him. Off in the distance, the sun was slowly sinking toward the horizon, coloring the sky with more deep and mesmerizing shades of summery pink, warm beachy orange and beautiful blue. At Allison's feet, tiny tropical fish darted through the water, and all felt right with the world. Everyone she loved was here. And she was ready to start her new life.

When she reached Zane, she gave her dad one more kiss before letting him join her mom. Then it was time to take the hand of the man who was her whole future.

"Hey there, beautiful," he whispered into her ear.

"You're not half-bad yourself." Dressed in a white shirt and pants, with the legs rolled up to midcalf, he was an absolute vision. She'd purposely asked him not to shave—she loved his late-day scruff. It was so sexy.

"Family and friends," Scott began. "We're gathered here today to witness the joining of Scott and Allison in matrimony. They will now share their vows."

Zane went first as they joined both hands and faced each other. She peered up at him, allowing herself to get lost in his eyes as he spoke. "Allison, you are my everything. You are my reason for getting up in the morning and the thing I am most thankful for when I lay my head down at night. I promise to always hold you in my heart, to support you in all your endeavors, and most of all, I promise to always love you."

"Allison, do you take this man to be your husband?" Scott asked.

"I do." She sucked in a deep breath and embarked on her own pledge. She'd practiced it one hundred times or more, but she'd wanted to get it just right. "Zane, you were once only a dream to me. And now you are my reality. When we're together, I feel nothing less than loved and cherished. When we're apart, I'm sad, but you're still there with me, in my head and in my heart. I promise to always keep you there, to support you in all your endeavors, and most of all, I promise to always love you."

"Zane, do you take this woman to be your wife?" Scott asked.

"Do I ever." Zane didn't wait for Scott to make the final proclamation. He gathered Allison in his arms, picked her up to her tiptoes and laid an incredibly hot kiss on her. It might not have been totally appropriate for a family gathering, but she was glad it was a taste of things to come. Their guests all clapped, hooted and hollered.

"Well, then," Scott said. "That makes you husband and wife."

After a few minutes of hugs and congratulations, everyone gathered to board the boat, with Zane and Allison last in line. They were actually hanging back a bit, taking their chance to wade through these warm waters, hand in hand, husband and wife. Zane pointed to the honeymoon cottage up on the hill. "I can't wait to spend the next few days with you up there."

"No storm this time."

"Not unless I manage to brew one up on my own."

Allison laughed and swatted Zane on the arm. "It's going to be perfect."

"It's where we fell in love," he said, pressing another soft kiss to her lips.

Allison knew then that all those years she'd lusted after Zane, it hadn't been love. Now it was nothing less. In fact, it was everything she'd ever wanted. "It absolutely is."

* * * * *

Dynasties:
Seven Sins

It takes the betrayal of only one man
to destroy generations.
When a hedge fund hotshot vanishes with billions,
the high-powered families of Falling Brook
are changed forever.

Now seven heirs, shaped by his betrayal,
must reckon with the sins of the past.

Passion may be their only path to redemption.

Experience all Seven Sins!

Ruthless Pride *by Naima Simone*
Forbidden Lust *by Karen Booth*
Insatiable Hunger *by Yahrah St. John*
Hidden Ambition *by Jules Bennett*
Reckless Envy *by Joss Wood*
Untamed Passion *by Cat Schield*
Slow Burn *by Janice Maynard*

Available May through November 2020!

WE HOPE YOU ENJOYED
THIS BOOK FROM

H HARLEQUIN
DESIRE

*Luxury, scandal, desire—welcome to
the lives of the American elite.*

Be transported to the worlds of oil barons, family dynasties,
moguls and celebrities. Get ready for juicy plot twists,
delicious sensuality and intriguing scandal.

6 NEW BOOKS AVAILABLE EVERY MONTH!

HDHALO2020

COMING NEXT MONTH FROM

⊕HARLEQUIN

DESIRE

Available July 7, 2020

#2743 BLACK SHEEP HEIR
Texas Cattleman's Club: Rags to Riches • by Yvonne Lindsay
Blaming the Wingate patriarch for her mother's unhappiness, Chloe Fitzgerald wants justice for her family and will go through the son who left the fold—businessman Miles Wingate. But Miles is not what she expected, and the white-hot attraction between them may derail everything...

#2744 INSATIABLE HUNGER
Dynasties: Seven Sins • by Yahrah St. John
Successful analyst Ryan Hathaway is hungry for the opportunity to be the next CEO of Black Crescent. But nothing rivals his unbridled appetite for his closest friend, Jessie Acosta, when he believes she's fallen for the wrong man...

#2745 A REUNION OF RIVALS
The Bourbon Brothers • by Reese Ryan
After ending a sizzling summer tryst years ago, marketing VP Max Abbott doesn't anticipate reuniting with Quinn Bazemore—until they're forced together on an important project. He's the last person she wants to see, but the stakes are too high and so is their chemistry...

#2746 ONE LAST KISS
Kiss and Tell • by Jessica Lemmon
Working with an ex isn't easy, but successful execs Jayson Cooper and Gia Knox make it work. That is until they find themselves at a wedding where one kiss leads to one hot night. But will secrets from their past end their second chance?

#2747 WILD NASHVILLE WAYS
Daughters of Country • by Sheri WhiteFeather
Country superstar Dash Smith and struggling singer Tracy Burton were engaged—until a devastating event tore them apart. Now all he wants to do is help revive her career, but the chemistry still between them is too hard to ignore...

#2748 SECRETS OF A PLAYBOY
The Men of Stone River • by Janice Maynard
To flush out the spy in his family business, Zachary Stone hires a top cyber expert. When Frances Wickersham shows up, he's shocked the quiet girl he once knew is now a beautiful and confident woman. Will she be the one to finally change his playboy ways?

YOU CAN FIND MORE INFORMATION ON UPCOMING HARLEQUIN TITLES, FREE EXCERPTS AND MORE AT HARLEQUIN.COM.

HDCNM0620

SPECIAL EXCERPT FROM

⟨H⟩HARLEQUIN

DESIRE

*After ending a sizzling summer tryst years ago,
marketing VP Max Abbott doesn't anticipate reuniting
with Quinn Bazemore—until they're forced together on
an important project. He's the last person she wants
to see, but the stakes are too high and so is
their chemistry...*

Read on for a sneak peek at
A Reunion of Rivals *by Reese Ryan.*

"Everyone is here," Max said. "Who are we—"

"I apologize for the delay. I got turned around on my way back from the car."

Max snapped his attention in the direction of the familiar voice. He hadn't heard it in more than a decade, but he would never, *ever* forget it. His mouth went dry, and his heart thudded so loudly inside his chest he was sure his sister could hear it.

"Peaches?" He scanned the brown eyes that stared back at him through narrowed slits.

"Quinn." She was gorgeous, despite the slight flare of her nostrils and the stiff smile that barely got a rise out of her dimples. "Hello, Max."

The "good to see you" was notably absent. But what should he expect? It was his fault they hadn't parted on the best of terms.

Quinn settled into the empty seat beside her grandfather. She handed the old man a worn leather portfolio, then squeezed his arm. The genuine smile that lit her brown eyes and activated those killer dimples was firmly in place again.

He'd been the cause of that magnificent smile nearly every day that summer between his junior and senior years of college when he'd interned at Bazemore Orchards.

"Now that everyone is here, we can discuss the matter at hand."

His father nodded toward his admin, Lianna, and she handed out bound presentations containing much of the info he and Molly had reviewed that morning.

"As you can see, we're here to discuss adding fruit brandies to the King's Finest Distillery lineup. A venture Dad, Max and Zora have been pushing for some time now." Duke nodded in their general direction. "I think the company and the market are in a good place now for us to explore the possibility."

Max should be riveted by the conversation. After all, this project was one he'd been fighting for the past thirty months. Yet it took every ounce of self-control he could muster to keep from blatantly staring at the beautiful woman seated directly across the table from him.

Peaches. Or rather, Quinn Bazemore. Dixon Bazemore's granddaughter. She was more gorgeous than he remembered. Her beautiful brown skin looked silky and smooth.

The simple, gray shift dress she wore did its best to mask her shape. Still, it was obvious her hips and breasts were fuller now than they'd been the last time he'd held her in his arms. The last time he'd seen every square inch of that shimmering brown skin.

Zora elbowed him again and he held back an audible *oomph.*

"What's with you?" she whispered.

"Nothing," he whispered back.

So maybe he wasn't doing such a good job of masking his fascination with Quinn. He'd have to work on the use of his peripheral vision.

Max opened his booklet to the page his father indicated. He was thrilled that the company was ready to give their brandy initiative a try, even if it was just a test run for now.

It was obvious why Mr. Bazemore was there. His farm could provide the fruit for the brandy. But that didn't explain what on earth Quinn Bazemore—his ex—was doing there.

Don't miss what happens next in
A Reunion of Rivals by Reese Ryan.

Available July 2020 wherever
Harlequin Desire books and ebooks are sold.

Harlequin.com

Copyright © 2020 by Roxanne Ravenel

HDEXP0620

Get 4 FREE REWARDS!

We'll send you 2 FREE Books plus 2 FREE Mystery Gifts.

Harlequin Desire® books transport you to the world of the American elite with juicy plot twists, delicious sensuality and intriguing scandal.

FREE Value Over $20

YES! Please send me 2 FREE Harlequin Desire novels and my 2 FREE gifts (gifts are worth about $10 retail). After receiving them, if I don't wish to receive any more books, I can return the shipping statement marked "cancel." If I don't cancel, I will receive 6 brand-new novels every month and be billed just $4.55 per book in the U.S. or $5.24 per book in Canada. That's a savings of at least 13% off the cover price! It's quite a bargain! Shipping and handling is just 50¢ per book in the U.S. and $1.25 per book in Canada.* I understand that accepting the 2 free books and gifts places me under no obligation to buy anything. I can always return a shipment and cancel at any time. The free books and gifts are mine to keep no matter what I decide.

225/326 HDN GNND

Name (please print)

Address   Apt. #

City   State/Province   Zip/Postal Code

Mail to the **Reader Service:**
IN U.S.A.: P.O. Box 1341, Buffalo, NY 14240-8531
IN CANADA: P.O. Box 603, Fort Erie, Ontario L2A 5X3

Want to try 2 free books from another series! Call 1-800-873-8635 or visit www.ReaderService.com.

*Terms and prices subject to change without notice. Prices do not include sales taxes, which will be charged (if applicable) based on your state or country of residence. Canadian residents will be charged applicable taxes. Offer not valid in Quebec. This offer is limited to one order per household. Books received may not be as shown. Not valid for current subscribers to Harlequin Desire books. All orders subject to approval. Credit or debit balances in a customer's account(s) may be offset by any other outstanding balance owed by or to the customer. Please allow 4 to 6 weeks for delivery. Offer available while quantities last.

Your Privacy—The Reader Service is committed to protecting your privacy. Our Privacy Policy is available online at www.ReaderService.com or upon request from the Reader Service. We make a portion of our mailing list available to reputable third parties that offer products we believe may interest you. If you prefer that we not exchange your name with third parties, or if you wish to clarify or modify your communication preferences, please visit us at www.ReaderService.com/consumerschoice or write to us at Reader Service Preference Service, P.O. Box 9062, Buffalo, NY 14240-9062. Include your complete name and address.

HD20R

IF YOU ENJOYED THIS BOOK
WE THINK YOU WILL ALSO LOVE

⬧HARLEQUIN

PRESENTS

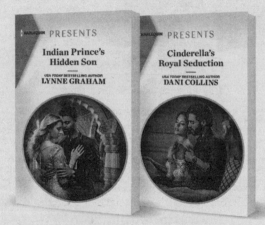

Escape to exotic locations where passion knows no bounds.

Welcome to the glamorous lives of royals and billionaires, where passion knows no bounds. Be swept into a world of luxury, wealth and exotic locations.

8 NEW BOOKS AVAILABLE EVERY MONTH!

HPXSERIES2020

Love Harlequin romance?

DISCOVER.

Be the first to find out about promotions,
news and exclusive content!

 Facebook.com/HarlequinBooks

Twitter.com/HarlequinBooks

 Instagram.com/HarlequinBooks

Pinterest.com/HarlequinBooks

ReaderService.com

EXPLORE.

Sign up for the Harlequin e-newsletter and
download a free book from any series at
TryHarlequin.com

CONNECT.

Join our Harlequin community to
share your thoughts and connect
with other romance readers!
Facebook.com/groups/HarlequinConnection

HSOCIAL2020

HARLEQUIN

Heartfelt or suspenseful, inspiring or passionate, Harlequin has your happily-ever-after.

With new books published
every month, you are sure to find the
satisfying escape you know you deserve.

SIGN UP FOR THE HARLEQUIN NEWSLETTER

Be the first to hear about great new
reads and exciting offers!

Harlequin.com/newsletters

HNEWS2020